The False River

Nick Holdstock

UNTHANK

First Published in 2019
by Unthank Books

Text Copyright @ Nick Holdstock 2019

ISBN 978-1-910061-56-5

Jacket Design by Robot Mascot
www.robotmascot.co.uk
Book Production and Typesetting by
Michelle Collin

www.unthankbooks.com

For Ryan

Contents

X

Half

Zoe stood at the end of the pier, looking back at the shore. Beyond the beach, above the road, she saw the line of hotels: white castles topped with flags, slightly blurred in her vision. She squinted, but they weren't just distant. They seemed to be retreating. As if she were at the stern of a ship that was calmly sailing away.

She touched her hair, then checked her watch. Perhaps Sam wasn't going to come. Perhaps, despite the way he'd sounded, things had not improved.

She leaned on the railing and wanted to shut her eyes. But the pier, for all its ironwork, did not feel like something to trust, not against so much water.

Five minutes, then she'd go; the London train was at half past.

She went to the telescope and pushed a coin in its slot. She bent and peered and turned it slowly. Windsurfers, waves, a dinghy. A single swimmer on his back. Then the grey of the water blurred to the yellow ochre of sand. More sand, then the freckled limbs of a woman without hair. The woman was wearing small dark glasses. She absently picked her nose.

Then she looked directly at Zoe with a stare that said, Fuck off. Zoe jumped and the telescope skipped to waves that lifted, hung, then fell. The woman had, of course, not seen her. If she moved the telescope back, the woman would be squeezing sun cream onto her arms.

She turned the scope till she was seeing down the pier. A pushchair, a rubbish bin, a cloud of candyfloss. She raised it and saw faces. White, black, lumpy, old, then, as the shutter dropped, the face of her half-brother.

He'd told her a year ago, just after he passed the bread, right as she started to butter.

'I'm using heroin,' he said.

'No you're not,' was all she could manage.

'Yes, I *am*.' He sounded bemused, as if she were not getting a really good joke.

She looked up, and he wasn't smiling. His palm cradled his chin as he gazed intently at her.

'Bullshit,' she said and looked in his eyes.

'Fine,' he said, pulled up his sleeve, pointed at two holes.

'They could be for tetanus.'

'You don't need two shots for tetanus.'

'Maybe you got a polio as well.'

Sam pointed at the top hole. 'This is from Friday.' He slid his finger down. 'This was yesterday.'

They were not the neat holes a nurse would have made. These were burgundy-coloured stains wrapped around a wound.

She sat back, about to speak, but then their food arrived.

He had the salmon. So did she. Their waitress said, 'Enjoy.'

'OK, I believe you. I believe you're fucking stupid.'

He picked up his fork. 'We're *all* fucking stupid.'

'Yes,' she said. 'We are.'

He shrugged and brought the fork to his mouth.

'Why are you telling me?' she said. But she was glad he had. 'Are you proud of this?'

'No.' He swallowed. 'But I'm not ashamed either. Look, it really isn't a problem. It's just that things have been shit. I hate my job.'

'Everyone does, that's no excuse.'

He sighed. 'I've only done it a few times. It's not like I *planned* to. I was at a party and this guy asked if I wanted to do some. I said I didn't, and he said OK, and then he shot up anyway. I've *never* seen anyone look as happy. I mean, he was in fucking *bliss*.'

'And that was what made you decide to do it?'

'Yeah,' he said, and she could hear a gentle lift of surprise. As if only now, in the telling, did he realise how it would hurt her. And she was touched by this. To know her feelings mattered to him.

'Do you know how *stupid* that sounds? This is how everyone gets addicted. Even nice, middle-class boys who earn forty grand a year.'

He moved a potato, looked at her.

'I'm sorry. I shouldn't have told you.'

'No,' she said. 'You shouldn't.'

She stared at his mouth, his lips. Of all the things she'd imagined him saying, none came close to this.

'Look. There are loads of people who take it regularly and still are able to function really well.'

'Like who?'

'The lead singer of The Charlatans. He's used heroin for years.'

'Who else?'

'Will Self. He took heroin regularly when he was a journalist.'

She shook her head. Looked at her food. This did not belong. Sam was good with cars, with fuses and switches. He had always been the sensible one, the one her wicked stepmother told her to be more like. When Zoe was six he stopped her putting her hand in the terrier's mouth. Later he was what stopped her from drinking bleach, from running away, from setting fire to their father's vintage car. By then she was in something like love. She suffered with the longing you feel for someone you see every day, who you live with, go to school or work with, someone with whom you are as intimate as you can possibly be.

Usually it was just a moth that fluttered round a bright bulb in her head. But sometimes, when there were other girls, she embarrassed herself. She never touched, or tried to kiss him – that led to nothing, not even hope – but there were times she laughed and lingered when Tammy or Gwen were close to kissing him. Only once had she gone further, when she hit Judith, whom everyone, for different reasons, thought deserved a slap the way she carried on.

Half. She used to roll the word round her mouth like a boiled sweet. Not a full, complete, whole brother. Someone who lacked fifty percent of whatever that was. And what about this other half? Was this portion that of a stranger, someone with whom you could do whatever you felt like? If something ever happened between them, would it only be half-wrong?

All this took an absurdly long time to die. But after five boyfriends, one abortion, four years studying Fine Art, Zoe understood that it had been only a silly infatuation that had no place in the head of a twenty-eight year old. It no more fitted with who she was now than his claim to be an addict. What he'd said made her so angry she wanted to make a scene in the restaurant. She'd throw her wine at him, kick over a chair, storm out of the place. This would definitely make her feel better. But it would not help.

'Look,' she said. 'Just be careful. I think it's really stupid. I think you'll get fucked up, and if I could think of a way to make you stop, I would. But I can't, so please. Don't share needles or overdose. Don't jump off the end of the pier.'

'OK.' He smiled. 'I won't.'

She felt as if he was saying goodbye, as if he was going on a journey to some place she'd never even heard of.

She cut her salmon; he rolled his sleeve down. He asked about her new job. She said it was good. 'But it's also weird. Continuity is one of those jobs that's supposed to be invisible. People only think about it if I make a mistake.'

'True.' He took a gulp of water. His throat gently bulged.

He asked if she was seeing anyone. She told him about Josh. 'He's a film-maker,' she said. 'We met on a shoot.'

'Great,' he said. She thought he meant it.

They ate raspberry panna cotta, drank espresso, and as they walked along the beach, the gulls could not stop crying. Never mind his words, the holes; she could not believe he was really doing this to her.

*

When she next saw Sam, four months later, the truth was too apparent. His face was drawn and pale and he seemed half-asleep.

'Big night?' she said, and her tone was wrong: sarcastic, accusatory, as if daring him to deny it.

'Yeah,' he said and stirred the cream into his mocha.

She looked away. The café was full of well-matched couples swapping sections from the *Observer*. None of them, she was sure, had ever taken heroin.

'Who were you out with?'

'Just some people. You don't know them.' He yawned. 'God, I'm shattered.'

'Where'd you go?'

'Round to a friend's. It was pretty good. But he has this really fat ginger cat that wouldn't leave me alone. It was jumping on my lap all night.' He laughed, and drank his third glass of water.

She knew this time there'd be no rolling-up of sleeves.

She stood up. 'Back in a minute.'

The light in the toilet was ultraviolet; her blouse glowed like a ghost. She turned on the tap, then sat on the seat. Pushed her mind into the water, the roar of it in the tiny space, its rush to get away. When she put her hands under the tap the water was painfully cold; as if it was from some frozen place where the only drug was fire. She looked at the backs of her hands. In the bluish light she could not see any veins, and that, of course, was the point.

When she came back Sam was asleep. His face had a sickly hue, as if he'd been poisoned. She sat and listened to the rasp of his breath as she finished her coffee. Once, he twitched, but did not wake, and there was little to say. Either they would argue. Or he would ask for money. He'd already told her he'd quit his job. 'I'd rather be freelance,' he'd said.

Zoe lifted her bag and coat. She gave him one more chance to wake up; then she walked away.

*

Six weeks later she moved in with Josh. His flat was twice the size of hers but had far fewer things. A CD rack, two shelves of books, not even many films. The sofa and chairs did not look used. Nothing was stained or worn.

The only truly personal items were the awards he'd won. These were arranged on a shelf in the bedroom, all facing the same direction, shining, without dust. She thought of him aligning them. Polishing their curves as if they were parts of some great and vital machine.

When he came home that night she said, 'Where's your *stuff*? You live like a monk.'

He shrugged. 'I don't know. I used to have some, but then there was a massive fire and I haven't had much since.'

'Well, you can have some of mine. I've got *loads*.'

'Great.' He made a face. Then they drank a Chilean red and he fucked her hard in the bath.

She spent the next day unpacking. After the clothes, the shoes, the books, there were four boxes of random stuff she didn't want but couldn't bear to throw out. Letters, menus, party hats, pink curly straws from six-shot cocktails that made her projectile vomit. There were also packets of photos, most taken with a red camera she'd called The Tomato. On the day she got it she'd used two rolls of film for the joy of pushing the button. She loved the happy click of the shutter. The pull of the spool as it bit the film and slowly dragged it on. There were pictures of their house, the sycamore, their cul-de-sac, her father standing in front of his car, smoking the pipe that killed him. There was only one picture of Sam because he'd been away on a hiking trip in Scotland. In the photo he was still wearing his rucksack and walking boots. Although he looked exhausted, he was smiling, obviously glad to see her. On the other side she'd written, 'The Great Explorer Returns!'

She put the picture back with the others. The only things she kept out were a large conch shell and her mother's jewellery box. These she placed on a small table by her side of the bed. She pushed the boxes to the back of the cupboard. Though there were now unmistakably two people living in the flat, the aesthetic was still minimalist. When Josh came home he looked around, and although he said, 'Where's *your* stuff?', she thought he was pleased.

*

Neither of them worked that week. After a long lie in they walked through weak winter sunshine to a café near Tower Bridge, which he said was the only place in London that had a Graef C800 grinder. The coffee was salty, and the barista was snide, but at least there was a friendly spaniel willing to sponge her affection. After lunch they walked along the river till they reached the National Film Theatre. He suggested they see what was on, then after they'd consulted the programme, that they see the Herzog documentary about hot air balloons.

Later, as they walked through the dusk, she looked at the lights that followed the river while he praised the sequence where mist had apparently moved through a valley like a phalanx of ghosts. She could not, in truth, remember the scene, but this did not need to be said. She enjoyed listening to him talk with such passion.

For the next six days this was their pattern, except on

Sunday, when they went to a Herzog double bill. Sometimes she felt tired from walking, and sometimes, as they sat in the cinema – she in a comfortable slump, he sitting so far forward he seemed on the verge of leaping into the screen– she closed her eyes and drifted in the sonorous wash of the German-accented English. But she was, without question, happy. They were living together.

When, a few weeks later, she received a text from Sam – saying that he'd be in London – Zoe did not reply.

*

Josh went to Hungary to film the stork migration. Zoe began work on a BBC drama set in the nineteen-eighties. She looked at actors' clothes, faces and hair, at the amount of water in glasses during restaurant scenes. She did this for ten hours a day, and as long as continuity was preserved, no one bothered her.

At night she sat in the flat and watched his small collection of films. She learnt about pelicans, cormorants, and swallows. She learnt about the mating habits of the lesser-crested grebe.

Josh called her regularly, though not every night. There was always a lot of noise in the background, the sounds of people with glasses whose levels didn't need to be checked. He told her they'd been mistaken for hunters; that their permits, which had been expensive, were rarely ever checked. He asked how she was, how the film was going, and although he sounded genuine, not once, during those three weeks, did he say he missed her. Zoe didn't want to sound pathetic. She limited herself to asking when he'd be back.

But one night, after three glasses of wine, she said she loved him. There was a pause and a woman laughed and then he said, 'Likewise.' Afterwards she finished the bottle and watched the condors fly.

She woke with a swollen tongue and a throb behind her eyes. She got up, went to the bathroom, drank water straight from the tap. It was like a cold hand stroking the inside of her throat and she felt she could never drink enough, and so she slurped and swallowed and then she felt she'd drunk too much. Her stomach felt so bloated she had to look at it to check. She'd imagined it distended, pregnant, and when she saw it was not she barked the start of a laugh which cut off after *ha*.

Zoe noticed the trophy on her way back to bed. It was the small turquoise plaque he'd won for his first film. The trophy wasn't on the shelf with the others. It was on the chest of drawers. It was missing a triangular piece the size of her fingernail.

She stared as if it were one of her organs. A kidney had snuck out. Zoe got on her knees, searched on the carpet, found the piece by the wall. She slotted it in and looked at the cracks that ran through the 'U' of his name. She swallowed and tried to remember. She could see herself picking up the plaque, turning it over in her hands like some ancient talisman. This she thought she had done. But she could not remember dropping or smashing the plaque. She vaguely remembered returning the plaque to the company of the other awards.

Something must have happened, and it didn't matter what. The plaque was damaged and it was her fault. What turned her stomach inside out as she rang her way through the Yellow Pages was the question of how he'd react. Most likely he would be angry. He would shout and call her names and this she could accept. But there was also a murmur of hope, a scene where he'd verbally shrug. Just a thing, just *stuff*, he'd say, and this possibility was what kept her from growing used to her fear.

Eventually she found a place in Shepherd's Bush. She rode on the West London Line, the plaque swaddled in cotton wool in a bag she kept on her lap. A fat man with flaking skin who could have been Syrian, Iranian, or Kurdish, but was, definitely, a Muslim – there were Arabic signs on the wall – took it from her and said, 'You come back. One hour.'

She went into Starbucks and ordered a latte with a cinnamon shot. She sat by the window and watched a man on the other side of the road. He was standing in the bus shelter, wearing a black hooded top. He was leaning, looking down at his feet, and although she saw six buses arrive, he never raised his head. Perhaps he too was hung-over. Perhaps it was no more than that.

When she went back to the shop, the owner shook his head and sighed.

'I am sorry,' he said, and showed her his palms. 'I tried my best but–'

'What?'

'As you can see–' He smiled, then put the plaque on the counter.

She bent and looked at it; the crack was barely hairline.

'Thank you,' she said. 'Thank you.'

'It is easy,' he said. 'So long as you have the pieces.'

She wanted to say more to him, to convey how much him fixing this meant. Instead she said, 'How much is that?'

He looked at her, then the trophy. He bit his lip. 'Ten pounds?'

*

When Josh next phoned her she didn't mention the trophy. She was going to, she had decided, but then he said he'd be home at the weekend, that he couldn't wait to get back. She was too happy to tell him. And if, as now seemed unlikely, he was annoyed with her, she didn't want him to have four days to think about it. But she was definitely going to tell him: carelessness was one thing; dishonesty was worse.

The right moment did not immediately present itself. Not while he was lapping at her, not while she was sucking him. Not while they ate Beijing duck; as he licked the plum sauce from her. It did not appear until next morning, when they sat and ate cold mangos while the Christians rang bells. The room was full of yellow light that jumped from the glasses and spoons. He had just finished telling her about when the storks rose from their nests on the chimneys, twenty or thirty, all at once, how they beat their wings and hovered, flew towards the sun until they disappeared. She said, 'That sounds incredible.' Then she put her hand on his. 'Listen, darling. There's something I need to tell you.' And as she'd thought, he wasn't angry. But he didn't say that it was just *stuff*. The only thing he said was, 'OK.' Then he stood and went to the bedroom. She heard him pick up the plaque, the creak of the bed as he sat.

By the time he came back she had cleared the table and washed-up.

'Is it OK?'

'Yeah.'

'I'm sorry.'

'It's fine,' he said, without reproach. As if nothing had happened. Neither that evening, or the next day, did he say or do anything to suggest he was annoyed. They went for a Thai meal; walked by the river; he held her while she slept.

*

She first knew something was wrong when she asked to see his footage. There was a beat of hesitation before he said, 'Sure.' It was neither a long or portentous pause; if she hadn't been paying close attention, she wouldn't have noticed it.

But it was enough to confirm her fears. As they sat and watched the storks, she began to feel sick.

Once she was aware of it, she heard it all the time. Whether she asked about work, his hair, if he wanted a coffee. As if he was reluctant to trust her with even these simple matters.

After ten days of this treatment, Zoe apologised again. Josh acted surprised. He claimed to have forgotten about it, and she tried to believe him. But the catch in his voice remained, an almost invisible stab. She wished he'd call her a clumsy bitch, start breaking things of hers. Even a degree of coldness would have been preferable. Then they could have it out. They could shout and bang the doors and either they would work it out or it would be over. Instead he continued to pretend he had forgiven her.

She suffered two months of this. She became withdrawn and only spoke to him when necessary. He, in his cruelty, kept asking what the matter was.

When Zoe received Sam's text, she replied at once.

*

Sam's face was in front of her and then it all went black. She straightened and looked down the pier but he was too far away. Just a person-shaped blob in the haze and it did not feel normal, or right, to watch him coming nearer. She turned, looked out to sea, at a ship that inched across. But this did not make her feel better. It was a pretence. And so, when he said her name, Zoe did not want to turn. He would see it in her eyes.

'Hey,' she said and then he hugged her. He was wearing a black wool coat that smelt of dry-cleaning; tears formed in her eyes. She blinked them back, said, 'Good to see you.'

'You too,' he said and smiled. His face lacked the pallor of their previous meeting; although his cheeks were still thin, it was a face she knew.

'What do you want to do?' she said.

'I don't know. Shall we get some food?'

'OK.'

'Great. Let's get some doughnuts.'

'That's not really *food*, is it?'

'No. But it's good.'

'Well then,' she said and headed towards the queue. Neither of them spoke as they waited; as they smelt the dough.

They ate on a green iron bench facing towards Eastbourne. The dough was soft and hot in their mouths; their lips were coated with sugar.

'These are amazing.'

'I know.'

They finished them and licked their fingers. They looked at the sea, the shore.

'Listen,' he said. 'I'm sorry. When you came down last time, I was a fucking mess. You were right. I couldn't handle it. I thought I could, but after a few weeks, I was doing it twice a day.'

'What about now?'

'It's better.'

'Does that mean you've stopped?'

He moved his head slightly, then stood. 'Shall we stroll?' He offered her his arm and she took it, and as they moved towards land the sun dropped from the clouds. A stripe of sea turned cornflower blue and she remembered an afternoon, too long ago, when they had walked on the Downs, their pockets stuffed with apples and bread and although it hadn't rained, the sunshine had been broken. The clouds made the sun rush over the slopes with almost desperation.

As they clomped along the pier she watched the distant band of sun. She wondered when it would catch them up. Either at the shooting gallery, or by those wooden scenes with holes that asked for smiling heads.

Sam asked about Josh, how things were going, and she said, 'I don't know. Not so good.' The patch of sun was now behind them, but she did not twist round. She preferred there to be no warning, for it to simply fall.

They passed the guns, the holes, a giant plastic ice cream that looked like Liberty's torch. At the end of the pier, she paused, certain it would break on them before they reached the shore. When it did not, she turned around. The sea was only grey.

'Let's get a drink,' she said.

They crossed the road then slipped into the Lanes. They walked down a street of small shops that sold second-hand books and records, vegetarian shoes, falafels, retro and vintage clothes, pipes and bags with cannabis leaves, the kind of shops she used to drift through only a few years before. What was different, what she did not recognise, was the students and teenagers who swarmed in and out as if they were the rooms of some grand mansion their parents owned. Their hair and clothes, even their faces – puffed with confidence and charm and words that came out right – none of these were feats she was capable of.

There were few other drinkers in the Font and Firkin. An old man stared at the mute television; a couple in late middle age who spoke in such low voices that what they were saying had to be secret or shameful. One of them, or both, were married, and as she watched the pint glasses fill, Zoe thought of their long afternoons, the ease with which they drank and deceived on maybe a daily basis.

They drank the first pint quickly. He told her about his new neighbours, a Polish man and his three daughters, none of whom left the house during the day, and who, as far as he knew, spoke virtually no English.

'What do they look like?'

'Beautiful. But sulky. Like they're dolls that were bought for someone for Christmas but never came out of their boxes.'

She laughed. 'I'd forgotten about that.'

'My mother never has.'

'How is she?'

He shrugged. 'Who knows? She's still in Australia, still with George. She still thinks she's going to be reincarnated as some kind of bird. Last time I spoke to her she said it was going to be a crane.' He sighed and raised his glass. 'To our crazy mother.'

She brought her glass to his. 'Your crazy mother.'

Zoe drank and thought of storks, their beaks; their wide and covering wings.

They finished their pints, and it was his round. She watched his back as it moved to the bar. He said something to the barman, who smiled, and even the adulterous couple paused to look at him. The woman had wispy hair and as she inspected Sam she pushed her hand through it, perhaps thinking it was his thick hair. Later, when the red-faced man climbed on top of her, she would shut her eyes, remember.

Sam brought back a different beer, something darker that coated her mouth with a sweeter taste.

'What's this?'

'Bombardier.'

'Cheers.' She gulped a mouthful, then, instead of lowering her glass, she drank from it again. It was the best beer she'd ever tasted; she wished she could drink it all the time, instead of water, and Sam looked at the huge clock on the wall that had roman numerals, not numbers, and when she said, 'Need to be somewhere?' she raised her eyebrows because, of course, he didn't. He was there, with her, and it was only twenty past seven; there were hours before her last train.

The adulterous couple left, either for his place, or hers, or some third, neutral space. She said, 'Same again?' and stood but instead he put his hand on his coat and suggested they get something to eat.

They ate in a busy tapas restaurant further down the street. They ordered squid, chorizo, olives, gambas and patatas bravas, and although these were wonderful – spicy, without being too hot – he hardly ate a thing.

'What's the matter?'

'You know how it is, you like the sound of something, and then when you get it, although it's good, it isn't how you imagined it.'

'Sorry.'

'It's not your fault.'

'I know but. What about dessert?'

'No, I'm okay. I had a big lunch.'

They sat in the candlelight, drinking their wine, and she ate a tiramisu that was so perfect she took only the smallest spoonfuls.

'You really should try this. It's heaven.'

'I don't think I could enjoy it as much as you. You look like you're about to pass out.'

He stood and went to the toilet. She scraped her spoon in the dish. When he came back, his face was damp, his eyes a little bloodshot.

'Are you OK?'

'Yeah, I just rubbed my eyes too much.'

He sat down and the waitress came over. They ordered coffees, which they drank, and afterwards the night outside had the raw smell of the sea. They walked on the seafront and her legs felt heavy; she wished he'd take her arm.

'When's your train?' he said.

'I'm not sure. Not for a while. We've got time for a drink.'

And so they walked and heard the sea. She saw him look at his watch but it didn't mean anything. There was no moon and the waves were only a lighter part of the dark.

They drank in a small pub on the way to the station. The paper on the walls was red and there were old jugs and basins hanging on hooks from the ceiling. They were by far the youngest people in the place, but she did not mind. She ordered a double Glenfiddich and they sat at a small table the colour of bronze that was made from something else. They talked about the pub, the people in it – whom she thought all looked like writers, the hunched but thoughtful way they sat – and the whisky used its hot, small hand to push her firmly into the hole marked 'drunk'.

She looked at Sam's mouth, his eyes. She did not want to go home to Josh and his passive-aggressive shit.

Her last train was at eleven-twenty. At eleven-fifteen she stood and said, 'We'd better go.' When they arrived, the platforms were empty. The train had been on time.

'You'd better stay at mine,' he said.

He raised his arm and an orange light floated out of the dark. They got in the taxi, and she missed the seat, and it was incredibly funny. The driver said something, and laughed, but Sam only shut the door then sat on the other side. The light went out and then they were going fast, too fast, down impossibly cluttered streets and she could not understand how they did not hit any of the cars that hemmed them in.

His flat was not as she'd expected. There was furniture,

a stereo, a flat screen TV: no spaces that suggested the selling of large, expensive items to provide cash for a fix. The place was tidy and clean, but still felt lived in, personal.

'Why don't you sleep in my bed?' he said. She did not disagree. She slipped off her shoes, then got on the bed, but only to be comfortable. She did not plan to sleep. They would lie together and talk. They'd drink more and it would be fun and when she leaned in to kiss him he would not pull away. This would all begin in a minute, once she'd had a rest.

When she opened her eyes, it was dark. She sat up. She was alone. She stood and moved toward something but it was only the wardrobe. She was dizzy and confused but eventually she found the strip of light that marked the bottom of the door.

Sam was lying on the sofa, all his clothes still on. He looked like one of those knights on top of a tomb who sleep the sleep of the just. She had not seen him like this, not since they were children and slept in bunk beds, him below, and her on top, until, without any warning, her stepmother had smirked and said it was time they had separate rooms.

As Zoe moved closer she saw his left sleeve was rolled up. On the table, on a copy of *GQ*, there was a spoon and a plastic lighter. Somewhere, close by, was a syringe, and the thought that he had put this in him, while she slept in the next room, made her bite her cheek.

But he was lying very still. She wasn't sure he was breathing. What if it was an overdose? His heart could have just stopped.

She bent to see, or hear his breath, and his lips were turned up to hers, and still her head moved down. His lips were warm with a salty taste and they parted enough. He opened his eyes and she looked in them as she moved her tongue in his mouth. They were glassy and unfocussed; his dry tongue was limp. He knew what was happening, but did not care. He was far away.

Zoe took her mouth from his. She went in the bedroom, put on her shoes, hurried out of the flat. She walked through the streets, and it was cold. Dawn took a very long time.

And Then

Once upon a time the universe began. There was nothing, and then something – energy, or maybe matter – and then there were pterodactyls and the diplodocus. Then there were the monkey men who saw the singing slab. Then there was an age of bronze, an age of iron, an age of silent dark. Then there were Crusades, and the wonder of Byzantium was pushed until it fell. Then there was the Renaissance, and then, after the Enlightenment, the dawn of capital. There were two world wars, and then a cold one, and then there were two people, a man and woman, who lived in Hyderabad, whose marriage was organized, and who then, for private reasons, made the great journey to Greater London, where they found refuge with an uncle who ran a paper shop. It was in the smaller of the two rooms above the shop that the man and woman made the child the man insisted be called Chandra, who, despite being second generation, never felt, as some put it, 'caught between two worlds.' Her mother's cooking and school lunches; the playground taunts and the murmur of home: none of these were contradictions. These things were of a single world that made sense even when boys hurled rocks at her mother as they freewheeled by. Some of them were excellent shots, and Chandra, only six weeks later, started her degree at Norwich. Three years passed, she graduated, and then she found a job in London. She rented a large room in a shared house with two cats, underfloor heating, and a front door with a small panel of stained glass whose main colours were green and red, and yes, when the sun picked its way through the clouds and branches, it did create emeralds and rubies on the beige stair carpet. She met men, four, not at the same time, except for those two weeks when she hadn't found a way to tell Sean, and all of this, the work, the men, the carpet jewels, her mother blind in her left eye, continued for three years until, at twenty-five, she stood on the platform at High Brooms while a February wind pushed chocolate wrappers round. The train was late. Or not coming. And there was something wrong with Britain. The way that people drank. The things they talked about. Multicultural or not, none of it seemed right, at least not for her right now. And this was why Geoffrey Wade and Jenny Mason, directors of Wade & Mason, Publishers (no poetry, plays, or short stories), received, in ten-point Times New Roman, a short letter informing them that she, Chandra Deepak, would be resigning because she was going to São Paolo to work with street children. And this was why there was a vacancy that Claire could apply for.

'Matthew, can I borrow your stapler?'

'Yes, Claire. Absolutely.'

Once upon a time the earth was slowly forming. Dust and rock soon ceased their spinning. Then there was an atmosphere and self-replicating things. Then the pyramids were raised, and then America was found. Then there was Hiroshima, Nagasaki, and then Margaret Thatcher exclaimed, 'We have become a grandmother.' And the first affair of Geoffrey Wade was massively, disastrously, a big balls-up, a *mess*. And this was not a great surprise, because cheating on one's fiancée was, like tennis or mah-jongg, a pursuit that required practice. How could he, on his first attempt, have known to organize his schedule so as to allow plausible periods when he was not at work or out with friends? How could he have known to keep a rack of shirts in his office cupboard that he, or his PA, took to the dry cleaners and that were never brought anywhere near home? He could not have. And so absences times scented shirts soon equalled suspicion. For the following three weeks it appeared that his marriage to Sylvia, if not quite *off*, was very far from on. But after tears and many flowers, the great train of their betrothal managed to reach the station. And Geoffrey knew he'd learnt his lesson. From then on, in spare moments, on the toilet, in the lift, he asked himself the simple question, *Are you being careful?* And the answer was almost always, *Yes*. There was only one *Perhaps* (Lesley, from Publicity, who did not seem very stable) and one definite *No*. He spent almost a month considering the dangers of sleeping with an employee that he had actual feelings for, during which time he and Chandra continued to meet on Friday afternoons in a hilariously awful hotel that had train tracks right beside it. Finally, one Monday morning, he asked Chandra to come into his office, and she did, looking meek and foxy, and he told her, without mucking about, that although their affair had been wonderful, the best thing in his life, it would have to end, because it wasn't fair on her, his wife, or their darling three-month-old son. And she had laughed and said, 'All right,' and though he was impressed by her depth of understanding he wished she'd been more upset. When he got her resignation two months later he thought it appropriate to go into his private bathroom to cry a little in tribute to her strength of character, force of will, and very soft brown feet. She was irreplaceable, but they would have to try, and, as always, there were plenty of applications from people who were well qualified to the same dull degree. He, as director, should have taken a leading role in the recruitment process. But the idea of replacing Chandra was really too depressing, so Geoffrey delegated the whole thing to Alasdair even though he was bound to mess it up. And this was why underqualified Claire was called for an interview.

'Bradford. What about you?'

'Nowhere really.'

'Really? Come on, Matthew, you have to be from somewhere.'

'Fine! We moved from London to Chicago when I was

five, and then to Singapore when I was twelve, and then back to England when I was sixteen.'

'That sounds great, you know, to get to live in all those places.'

'I don't know, Claire. Maybe.'

Once upon a time, Qin Shi Huang, first emperor of China, had an unemployment problem. And so, to keep order, he decreed that great walls be built. And then, two thousand years later, another wall was built in Berlin, and when Alasdair was told his mother had Alzheimer's the large consulting room with the peach wallpaper was not big enough to hold his vast and doubled grief. It wasn't because they were close: she only lived half an hour's drive away but they met only once a month, and when they did it was always pleasant but never the kind of powerful, intense experience he saw other Sons and Mothers having. The greater cause of grief for Alasdair was the knowledge that something (in this instance, his mother) would soon be removed, something that had stood between him and death. Because that was when he accepted that he would really die. Death, as horde or lone assassin, could scale his wall at any time: next year, tomorrow, now. And he was being stupid, selfish. His mother was dying. It was happening all the time. Even while he sat with her, held her hand, used words in a brittle way, her supply of brain cells was slowly running out. And everyone at work knew this. For the first few weeks they lapped him with waves of sympathy. A smile at the copier, a held-open door, a supposedly unwanted doughnut gifted to his desk. But they had their own healthy lives that just continued on. How can he, apropos of nothing, tell them she no longer knows his name or that he is her son? If only Jenny or Matthew would ask. Then he would not feel so bad. And although Claire didn't ask either during her interview, and although he didn't therefore tell, when he asked her to roleplay a situation in which a colleague had recently been bereaved she was sympathetic and kind and displayed none of the confusion, suspicion or outright hostility shown by the other candidates. And this was not the only reason he gave her the job.

'Claire, have you had lunch yet?'

'No, I've got to finish this.'

'No you don't. Look at the sky. It's sunny. It's sort of warm. Let's go sit in the gardens.'

'But I have to give this to Geoffrey.'

'Sure. But he's gone to lunch with some woman, and, judging by the looks of her, there's no way he'll be back by four.'

'Very funny. He's married.'

'So's Elizabeth Taylor.'

'Look, Matthew, even if you're right, it will still take me two hours to finish this.'

'And what's the time? Quarter past one. You've got loads of time. So come on. There'll be squirrels.'

Once upon a time Jesus Christ was born. He said something

about love, and then the soul of man was saved. And then there was Auschwitz, Srebrenica and Matthew is not sure that he likes children's books. There is something underhand about them. With a normal book, for adults, the ideas can be ignored. But kids don't really have a choice, they can't help but absorb the ideas in children's books. The vapid, banal platitudes about stroking kittens and not stealing jam just get sucked up by them, and that's why kids are scary. They get force-fed propaganda they don't know how to use. They could be made to do anything. Maybe that's why they have those creepy stares that make him feel as if they see inside his head and are going to tell everyone what they have found. And this never used to matter. When Matthew joined Wade & Mason, five years ago, they were only publishing several children's titles a year. Now, after the success of *Paws*, almost half his job involves the bloody things. He cannot think of a way out; *Paws in Paris*, the tenth book in the series, is due next month. But then Chandra does a bunk to South America. Which leaves fantasy in a mess, because Deena can't delegate, and Alasdair is bloody useless. So when Matthew says to Geoffrey, 'Will you let me take it on?' it almost seems reasonable, except that fantasy sells half as much as children's, which makes it a demotion, and why would anyone want a demotion? But he has dealt with Geoffrey's wife when she's been difficult. When Sylvia has said she does not believe that he is in a meeting. When she has threatened to come in. On these occasions he has managed, by way of his nice vowels and preppy hair, to calm and persuade her not to. And this is why Geoffrey says 'Alright'. This is how Matthew ends up sitting next to Claire.

'But what else is there? Even if you don't believe in God, and I don't, what other kind of commitment can you make except for getting married? What else are you going to do? Get a mortgage together? Is that the best our secular but money-worshipping society can do? If it is, we're *fucked*.'

'Wow, Matthew. No wonder you've been married twice.'

'What, because I'm crazy?'

[she laughs] 'No. Because you take it seriously.'

'Well, I once saw this film with Donald Sutherland in which he played this really strange priest who delivers a wedding speech about how we shouldn't feel bad if our marriages don't work out, because getting married is just a way of trying our best. It's an optimistic gesture, and that's the main thing.'

'OK, maybe you're not that serious about marriage.'

'No, no, I am. Really.'

'OK. What was the film called?

'No idea. It was on TV one night. I was really drunk.'

Once upon a time the Muslim armies conquered Persia. Then there was the Six-Day War, and Deena cannot believe that Matthew has been put in charge of fantasy. Maybe he's charming, and maybe he's funny, and maybe he knows fuck-all about fantasy literature. The only book he's ever mentioned is

The Lord of the Rings, and that was only after the shitty films came out. He has always, at parties and meetings, spoken of the genre with a lilt of condescension. She and Chandra built that section. They were the ones who sat and talked and read while the cleaners worked in the evenings. They were the ones who found the truly visionary stuff that bent every rule. They published the Dark Sun series; they published *Wild Fire*. And maybe fantasy only sells a third of what those stupid *Paws* books do. But the work they publish is excellent; it will last. And Matthew will fuck it all up. In the last two weeks he's rejected three brilliant manuscripts. Deena does not hate Chandra, Deena is not angry. But the fact remains: all this is Chandra's fault. And so what if Claire is nice and friendly; she seems like the kind of creature that defers to men. Every time Deena glances at her and Matthew Claire is leaning towards him as he speaks, as if his voice is some incredible fragrance whose source she has to get closer to. And this is not just bad for the books, it is also bad for the office. They are a waste of gossip. If only Jenny wasn't sick. If she was here she'd stop their nonsense taking over.

'Yeah, I saw it last night. I thought it was really good.'

'What did you like best?'

'The horses, they were really funny. Maybe they were too rude sometimes, but I really believed in them. They said the kind of things I expect a flying horse with two heads to say.'

[he laughs] 'Do you really have expectations about that kind of thing?'

[she also laughs] 'Sort of. I mean, it all made sense. None of it sounded stupid. Except for maybe that stuff about the ring that remembers every finger it's been on.'

'Oh, I liked that. Didn't you think that was romantic?'

'No, it was silly.'

'OK, so what *do* you think is romantic? Candlelight? A string quartet? Mr. Darcy with red roses in a limousine?'

'I don't know. Maybe.'

'What about dinner in a small Italian restaurant that has good vegetarian options? Would that be romantic?'

'Yes.'

'And if you were eating with someone who really likes you? Would that be romantic?'

'Yes.'

'So if you were free, and that person asked you, would you meet him at Ulivo, on Stoke Newington Church Street, at eight thirty tonight?'

[she laughs] 'Yes!'

'OK. See you then.'

Once upon a time the French lost at Agincourt, and then there was 9/11, and when Jenny's in her corner office all the space feels wrong. Vertigo, but inverted: it is looking up she fears. The ceiling, and the floor above, and so on, to the roof. After that, just empty air and falling up so fast. Up to space where it is cold and she will suffocate. She first felt it two months ago, and at the time she had blamed the veal; it was that sort of disquiet, the sense of wrong increasing even though there wasn't pain or any urge to vomit. That day she'd sat at her desk and talked into her phone to no one at all until it passed. The second time, three days after, she had to lie on the floor, facedown, counting, breathing, reciting in an inner voice the names of all the books that Asimov had written, co-written, or merely edited. And gravity is not some big machine that can just break down. She knows this. There is no chance of it failing, no chance of her being taken into vast and roaring nothing. She knows that her brain is wrong. She only feels this way when she is in her office. When she is outside, unprotected, everything unfolds as normal. The sky only evokes one feeling: a sense of limitless expansion.

'Hey.'
'Hey.'
'Are you OK?'
'Yeah. You?'
'Yeah.'
'You look really nice.'
'So do you.'
'What time is it?'
'About nine. Why? Do you have to be somewhere?'
'No.'
'Good. Because I think we should stay here all day. I mean, it looks horrible outside.'
'Yeah, I can see that.'
'And it's not as if we'd be able to go for a long walk down

the Embankment, and then have several bottles of wine. In this weather' [his hand flicks the blind, and sharp sun enters] 'it would be awful.'

'Awful.'

'Nasty.'

'Horrid.'

'I already said that.'

'No, you didn't, you said 'horrible'.'

'Close enough.'

'Let's not talk anymore.'

'Agreed.'

'Fine.'

'Have you got any juice?'

'So now we're talking?'

'Maybe.'

'All right. Orange or apple?'

'Apple.'

'No.'

'OK, orange.'

'Nope.'

[she laughs] 'Are you always this funny in the morning?'

'You're laughing.'

'It's not my fault. I'm just happy.'

'Really? Me too. But seriously, I'm really hungry. There's a Polish bakery near here. I could be back in twenty minutes.'

'I'll come with you.'

'Are you sure?'

'Yeah.'

'Great, OK, let's go.'

[He gets out of bed. Claire does not]

'What is it? Changed your mind?'

'No.'

'Do you want me to dress you?'

'No.'

'So what's the matter?'

'Sorry, I'm being really silly. I'm shy. I don't want you to see me.'

'That's all right. I'll be in the lounge.'

'Thanks. I'm sorry.'

'It's OK. See you in a minute.'

Once upon a time London had a plague, then a fire, and Sylvia knows where Geoffrey puts his dick. There was his personal trainer, his accountant, then Chandra; heaven knows how many interns. And she makes a show of minding. There is the divorce to think of. But in actual fact, she's glad. Their marriage was a good trade (his money for her status), and there is always someone who wants to screw the posh wife of the boss. Alasdair, that mope, was fine; Chandra was a lovely girl with remarkable hands. Sylvia sucked Matthew once, and she wonders when he'll follow up because he was big. Probably not until he's finished with that silly new girl who has bad hair.

'Claire?'

'Yes darling?'

'What do you want to do this weekend?'

'I don't mind.'

'Do you want to go to the cinema? The new Terry Gilliam is out.'

'OK, great.'

'Or do you want to go to the V&A? Alasdair says there's a new John Tenniel exhibit?'

'That sounds lovely. We could have lunch at Artichoke.'

'Or we could spend the weekend in a listed cottage. It has a log fire, views of woods and sheep, and it's called Little Midge.'

'That sounds wonderful! Whose is it?'

'Gareth's. He was my best man.'

'The first time?'

'That's right. So which one do you want to do?'

'All of them. I can't decide.'

Once upon a time the good ship *Titanic* sank. And then Geoffrey's doctor phones. Alasdair must see his mother; Jenny starts to leave the ground. Deena is killed by a tractor; Chandra is declared a saint. And Matthew, fucking Sylvia, feels sort of, kind of, *bad*.

The Embrace

There is no excuse: buildings have windows, roofs and stairs; roads have lorries and cars. In her house there are knives, pills and bleach. There is a gas oven. If after two years, Heather is not dead, it is because she's a coward. All she does is say her prayers before she goes to bed. *Dear no one, dear nothing, let something burst while I sleep. It does not need to be my heart, just an artery.*

But every night her body fails her. Every day, she wakes.

She gets up and goes into the bathroom where there is a large window. *Open it and fly beyond*, say several bars of soap. Why is it these things that speak? Why not the shampoo?

She sits on the toilet, water leaves her. She flushes and puts down the lid. What was a toilet is now a step, which leads to another, as it does on a scaffold. She climbs up and opens the window; the sky is full of white clouds except for a gap that beckons. It will close, and never reopen, and so she must hurry. All she need do is lean out; gravity will help.

The problem is that the hole is over a cloud, which is above a roof, a window, a stretch of wall, a plaque that says '1898'. There is then another window, an intervening branch, and finally, the schoolyard, or part of it, a narrow stretch between portacabin and fence, and soon a bell will ring.

Heather climbs down, then turns on the shower. She takes off her underwear, waits – the water may still be cold – then gets underneath. The water is warm, then properly hot, and it does not take long to wash. Soap on her face, soap under her arms, soap between her legs. Once this chore is done, she can close her eyes. Focus on water meeting her skin, the paths it takes down her back and arms; the glide of it down her legs. She does not think, hear words, see pictures. She is held by water.

When she was growing up her parents' house didn't have a real shower, just a forked plastic tube stuck onto the bath taps. She didn't have a proper shower until she was nine. That was the year she decided to stop being fat. She gave up biscuits and sweets. She made her mother drive her to the pool each morning. There she travelled up and down her lane, upheld and surrounded by water she kicked and pushed aside.

Heather stands under the shower till the water runs cold. When she gets out, she is shivering, and there must be clean clothes in the drawer. But it will take too long to look, and she is cold, so she puts on yesterday's clothes. She dries her hair then goes to the hall mirror and puts on the wig. It is made from nice, human hair, and she thinks of the woman it came from – tall, beautiful, but completely bald – and a laugh rises in her. Through the lungs, past the trachea, up and out like some billiard ball she has only this chance to expel.

At home, it is safe to do this. She does not do so in public, not any more, partly because her laugh is neither glad nor infectious, just a craven gulping of breath. The other, greater reason is that people seem to be of the opinion – she knows, because she was one of them – that if Sofia, your daughter, your flaxen-haired six-year-old, is killed in front of you, this is the end of laughter. If this happens, you must turn your face to the wall. Life cannot continue.

'But,' says Heather, and opens the door. Then quickly closes her mouth. Because someone could be in the stairwell. Except this is the point of speaking: to communicate. If she meets someone in the corridor or on the stairs she will tell them how awful she feels. So what if they don't want to hear. They need to be reminded that years of effort can vanish in a second. That everything you worked for, everything you valued – the promotion you worked eleven-hour days to get; the man you made dump his fiancée – can suddenly be worthless.

Unfortunately Heather sees no one on the way out. She must remain as mute as those women in novels of misery set in the 1950s, those Canadian or Irish martyrs that cannot escape their abusive fathers or husbands, their strict communities. No single shaft of light – not the song of a bird or a winter sunset or the pleasure offered by hot water and fingers – can enter their fictional lives.

Bullshit, she thinks, and laughs again. Despair is not like that. It is crying till you vomit, it is being cut from inside. It is screaming to drown out your thoughts. But even when one's capacity for happiness seems wholly amputated, even then there are brutal moments when a cat unwinds from a tree and before you can think you have knelt and run your hand through its fur. And though the feeling at such times is neither bright nor shining, it is still a balm.

She walks to the end of her street, then stops. How fast the cars on the road. Like hurry given a shape. Flashes of blue, red, sometimes yellow, and always those black taxis. Their orange, evil eyes. She looks left, then right, and the street seems clear, but still she walks on further, to the pedestrian crossing, although it is the wrong direction. There she presses the button and waits while others simply cross. Only when the green man appears does she step out. It has only added a minute to her journey, but it may be decisive. She may be too late.

She walks along the edge of the park and does not see autumn, the copper leaf carpet, the bare branches against a sky so blue it screams. She is walking so fast her feet hurt, but what she should do is run. Because sometimes they are let out early, sometimes she is too late. Then her head feels as if it's under a pillow that someone is pressing down. She is suffocating, cannot breathe, but it is worse than real suffocation: that at least would end.

Her shoes are loud on the pavement. People stare, they laugh. Not at her but with whoever they're talking to on their phone. And it always delighted Sofia that someone who was not there could still speak. She thought it funny that her father was so far away it would take 24 of their bus rides to reach him, in Canada, where it was cold, and wolves lived on the streets.

By now, the school bell should have rung. What if it is broken, or someone forgot? What if the children have already been picked up? Then she will have to endure the afternoon, evening, night and morning with the pillow over her face. And it will be only her fault.

'You stupid cow,' she says, and two girls turn. They see nothing interesting: just a middle-aged woman in tears. Pointless to cry, useless to scream, the milk, the blood, was long ago spilt. The schoolyard will be empty; Sofia is dead.

Heather passes the newsagents, dry cleaners, and chip shop. She presses the button that stops the murderous traffic, the button that is metal, cold and keeps her fingerprint. And as green gives way to amber she notices the women in coats and scarves, the two fathers by the school gate. When the light turns red she steps forward and knows a zephyr of relief. A lessening of pressure, a needful breath, and then relief is displaced by guilt. She means no harm, she *does* no harm and yet she knows this is a mistake. *Be true to thine own suffering:* that is what people expect. If she lifts the load from her shoulders, breathes normally, laughs, smiles, she betrays Sofia's death. She is not supposed to feel pleasure: it insults the pain.

She looks at her watch. Five minutes remain. She puts a cigarette in her mouth, then lights it. As she moves the lighter to her pocket, she burns her hand on the top, and without thinking, lets go. As she bends to retrieve it, she places a hand on her head. She doesn't think she needs the wig, and only wears it from habit. In the six months she's been coming to the school, no one has stared at her with suspicion. No one has noticed her, not the teachers, especially not the parents. They are not vigilant for paedophiles and kidnappers. They have come for that moment when their child spots them, when they are recognised, when someone is happy to see them.

The school bell rings, but it isn't a bell, just an electric line, a blade that falls, cutting *before* and *after.* To the children it means that something is over, to the parents, the teachers, that something continues. Back to home and lunch and TV and this is what the children run towards, not their parents, waiting with hands in pockets or talking on phones and here and there, the sensible, with arms fucking outstretched. The children burst out the doors and are told not to run but still they streak across her vision, a pink blur, a green, and their voices fill the air like an argument of birds. There is a hope that lives in the scene, something that starts to loop her intestines round its fingers, thumbs and toes, pulling, then yanking, and once or twice, at the start of this term, she had to go off and vomit.

Because there is only one girl here who matters. She is five, maybe six, her name is Tessa, and she looks nothing like Sofia. But resemblance is not in the hair or face, but a light that lives in the person entire. Though Tessa has black hair, not blonde, and is a slighter, doll-like girl than Sofia, she is still her echo. She is stood in the centre of the playground. She cannot see her mother, whose blue Volkswagen is nowhere in sight, but it is too early to worry: there are still many children running, laughing, moving in her orbit.

Heather steps close to the chain-link fence, then presses her face against it. Though she is only inches nearer, she no longer sees the fence. There is nothing to interrupt the quotidian sight of a girl in a playground full of boys and girls, a girl who is not levitating or speaking Creole or doing anything unexpected. She is looking at her feet while hopping, first on her left foot, then on her right, and it is banal, and it is a wonder. Heather cannot see the look on her face, but she can imagine it. In some other, better, former life she went to galleries and stared at shepherds and magi gathered round a holy infant. Pictures that seemed dull, repetitive, and when she herself became a mother, her expression was far from beatific. Fourteen hours of labour left her weeping, drained and angry, at the doctors for not speeding things up, at her body for taking so long. After the birth she was depressed for months, but she pushed herself through the days. And she loved Sofia, of that she has no doubt. But when you are constantly having to take care of a child – to make sure she is properly fed, warm, safe, and happy, that she is not ill, that she has toys and books and games and friends and that these friends and their parents can be trusted, that there are no wine glasses or medicine left within reach, that the dog she is petting is not bad-tempered, that the locks on her window are closed – when you are solely responsible for such things, because the father has decided to stay in Canada with a woman he met on a train, there is rarely the time or energy to feel the undiluted awe she feels while watching Tessa. She has not even spoken to this girl, has never been closer than ten feet to her, but still the sight of Tessa tilting her head to watch the flock streaking above, the slow turn of her head to track them as they circle, is enough to make Heather giddy. And this is sick, horrible, unquestionably *wrong*. This joy would not exist unless she were otherwise miserable. It only exists because Sofia saw a husky on the other side of the road and was so excited that she pulled her hand from Heather's and dashed into the road. It only exists because the taxi was going so fast and screams do not stop cars.

And when strangers – may God forgive them – ask her if she has a child, she says that she does. She has a child who died. She does not have Tessa, who is not Sofia, but for five seconds or a minute or ten, she borrows the girl with her eyes and her heart. The burden lifts and she laughs and laughs without ever opening her mouth. It is a purely physical kind of relief. The pain is still there, the wound is still there, but briefly it is not felt.

She should not come. She has tried not to, she has. But it is like trying to stay outside in the cold when you know there is a warm place. She can almost lay down, close her eyes, but there is the glow from the fire. The smile on the face of Tessa who is chewing her sleeve. Without this, she could find the courage, or perhaps despair, that would let her find sleep.

The playground begins to empty. Tessa looks around,

then down at her shoes, and then begins to walk. Her black shoes skip between the painted white lines on the ground, and at first it seems like she is playing some private game where the lines are like ropes on an obstacle course, or must not be stepped on because they would say Ouch. Then she is running, hurting the lines; she must have seen her mother. A tall woman with light brown hair whose long nose and thin cheeks give her face a sharpness that is probably undeserved. Even when she looks exhausted, beaten by life, she hugs and kisses Tessa. Which does not prove she is a good mother. But it suggests love.

Whatever Tessa is running towards, it is not her mother. This is clearly one of those actions caused by that energy which builds in a child till it demands release. When they hurl the doll against the wall, sweep the dishes from the table, launch themselves into the road. Though there are other adults stood at the gate, none are waving or smiling. No one is paying attention. Tessa is a toy wound up too far and soon the key in her back will slow and she will come to a halt. But she does not. She runs round a green circle painted on the ground, follows the back of a snake. If anything, she seems to be getting faster, as if the gears and cogs that move her are out of control. Something as fragile and precious as Tessa should not be moving so fast. How little it would take – a hard surface, a metal corner – for her to permanently stop.

And Tessa has finished running the snake. She is aimed at the gate. Her shoes are shiny, black with a strap and what if she. What if she, and it was an accident. If she did, if she was. Then Heather probably could. A window or a truck or bleach; the gas turned up to mark nine.

She watches the blur of Tessa's shoes. They shine and wink in the sun. Running, running, moving faster. Tessa reaches the gate. Where she is sure to be stopped by a teacher or parents. But the teacher has her back turned; the two parents are whispering, paying no attention. Tessa is the unstoppable force in search of an immovable object. She is on the pavement. Moving between parked cars.

Tessa's scream is a knife in their ears. It means they have failed. For a child to be making such a noise suggests that every adult, whether parent, teacher or passer-by, has failed to do the basic, vital task of protecting the vulnerable.

Except that Tessa is not screaming in pain. She is just surprised to be in the arms of a stranger. Perhaps she believes what Heather is saying. That she is safe, she is safe.

And Heather should put her down. In a moment, she must. But Tessa's hair smells of coconut. Her forehead is too soft. Heather knows she is not holding Sofia. She knows her daughter is still dead. But feelings are different from truth. Holding Tessa is like holding Sophia, not the same, but close. She shuts her eyes and floats in a moment that is barely the present, so little does life intrude.

Seven in the Light

You stand on a London street in 1924. The air is thick, you can barely see; the people who pass by are scarcely visible. There is only time to catch a glimpse of a nose, a cheek of beard, an intimation that this man – Gerry? Gerald? – is furious. The next person is walking more slowly. You perceive an earring, a curve of lipstick, the memory of an assignation beneath Lambeth Bridge. Then she is gone, still mostly a stranger, back into the dark. Perhaps the problem is that these people move too fast. You need someone stationary on which to shine your light.

You spy people in a ground floor room of a Georgian house on the other side of the road. From this vantage point they are merely silhouettes that tease. You must cross the street, approach the window, press your face against the glass. Now, when your light is close, they can be truly seen. Four men and three women are dining together, none of them much older than the century. They are well-dressed, they seem like old friends. In the general illumination, as you look at each face, you catch hints of madness, love, and incest. With whom should you begin?

You look at Reggie, cutting his terrine into one, two, three slices, and you see a man acting with care. Next he should transfer toast to his plate, but instead he first shifts his wine glass forward by two inches. He is worried that a silly accident will ruin everything. If, at the end of the evening, when the others have gone, there is a nasty red stain on the cloth, he will not be able to kneel, produce his heart, then present it to Audra. His heart is tired of its box. His heart wants to be in her hands.

There was a night three months ago that seemed like it could only end with her saying *Yes*. He arrived early, before the others, and spoke to her wittily for nearly ten minutes: she must have laughed at least twice. During that dinner she had eyes for no one else, not even her brother Ian. When Reggie recited stanzas by Shelley she brought her gloved hands together, as if to say, *And so shall we be joined.* She was virtually in a white dress, reciting her vows, when stupid Maude choked on a bone. Her cow's eyes bulged and had it not been for Ian's fist striking her back the evening might have been ruined. After that there was no question of a proposal. The following day Audra went to the Levant for a month. Since her return she has been distant, inscrutable, as if behind a veil.

But tonight the signs are good. They haven't even finished their entrees and Audra has looked at him three times (and maybe more, he can't be sure, he doesn't want to stare). As the last morsel enters his mouth Audra pivots to her left, treating him to what is certainly look number four. Her lips part and then there is a moment of ventriloquism. He hears the words he wants to. And then passes the salt. But if her look-count reaches ten, he will definitely propose. If not, he'll climb the stairs to the attic, open the bureau, unfold the—

'Reggie, what's the name of that chap, you know, the one who wears those awful tweeds?'

Freddie's words are bottles breaking. He's always such an oaf.

'Do you mean Simon?'

'That's right. Strange fellow. Can't look you in the eye.'

Reggie nods and glances at Audra. She is not looking at him. She is staring at her plate in a bubble of gloom. But as you inspect her face the air around her brightens. Of course she knows about Reggie's feelings. His infatuation. Because that's all it is. Reggie is charming, kind, and generous; but very much a boy. A few lines of white piping and his navy jacket could be a sailor suit.

But though Reggie is an infant, he's not the worst of them. Freddie is telling her brother Ian a story that began as a cautionary tale about the evils of gambling, but has become an excuse for him to relate one of his bawdy anecdotes about When He Was In Tahiti. She wonders if Freddie's slept with anyone but whores. When he touches himself does he imagine her face? Because in their last year at Cambridge there was That Afternoon on the banks of the Cam. The two of them drank a bottle of Bollinger and then lay down to wait for the others. Freddie must have thought she was sleeping. She didn't mind his paws on her face, her neck. She allowed his fingers to trace shaking circles on her chest. But when they slipped lower, when his fingers fumbled, then she had to stop him. Back then she thought this mattered. It was before Cairo, before Mustafa, the olive taste of his—

'Freddie, pass the sauce boat, you can't have it *all*!'

Stare at Linus, consider his features, firm its line into focus. Know that he really wants to shut dear old Freddie up. There's only so much a chap can swallow, especially if the fellow happens to be one's future best man. Linus doesn't want Freddie to make a fool of himself. Because the other guests will say, 'A splendid wedding. Truly fine. But you have to wonder what made Linus choose someone like *that*.' And these things They say are what make the difference when They um and aah about whether to place you in a middle or upper rank. Linus is not afraid of facts. The world will take good care of him, but it asks certain things: to respect the lines his fathers drew; to praise God and Industry; to take due care in speech and deed; to marry and produce heirs; in short to know the grand scheme and his place in it. To progress he must square his shoulders. Not just for himself, but for Elizabeth. She sits next to him, a tall, pale porcelain ornament that must be protected. About this the doctors have been clear. What Linus doesn't understand is why she gets so anxious. If anyone knows, it must be Audra. They were at school together and have always been friends. If only he could have a proper talk with her. But Reggie, her shining knight, will permit no one else to approach. Why can't the poor fool see that his courtship is doomed? Freddie is right about one thing: Audra only has eyes for her Sapphic cousins. That scene in the Strand last year proved it beyond—

'Don't take *all* the sauce,' says Freddie.

Audra sighs. 'Freddie, there's enough for *both* of you.' She looks at Reggie, shakes her head. And Reggie thinks, *look five*.

'That's right, listen to mummy,' says Ian and his laugh is a bright sound that commands attention. He looks at his sister, thinks, *If it were allowed*. If there was no God, no parents. No society. If he and Audra were still children playing on the sands of Margate while the adults dozed. If they could climb aboard some boat that would float them far away from customs that shouldn't be laws. If they could grow up all over again on some tropical island. Some place where they could be free from all the eyes.

Yet he suspects that even if this happened he'd still have no chance. The needle of her character will always swing to true north. No matter that it has wobbled, swung east to a vulgar woman, west to that man in Cairo. By 30 she'll be Mrs Someone Else. If he is ever going to have her, it must be soon. A few drops of laudanum is all that—

There's shouting in the street behind you. Three people, with heavy footsteps, quickly step from the shadows. Turning late, you gather fragments, sparks. A mouth with a missing incisor, a name – Celeste – and the men's intention. *Plenty of gin* is all you hear. Then they are returned to the dark.

As you turn back to the window Elizabeth starts to speak.

'May I have some water? Thank you,' she says. She picks up the glass, peers through it, sees the blur of Audra glance at Reggie (whose lips shape a word). She inspects the apparent nothing of her water glass's contents. The lie of its transparency. Only if the brightest light strikes the liquid will it reveal itself. Even then, it slips from view, tries to hide itself.

She wants to slip beneath the table. In that murk of crumbs and dust she could be safe. There she'd see no faces. Skin wouldn't peel back to show clotted loves and hates. If only she could live in darkness. Must she blind herself?

'Cheer up Maude! It's not a wake.'

'That's true,' says Reggie. 'If it were, my glass wouldn't be empty.' He looks at Audra – this is, after all, *her* house – and when she looks at him, and smiles, he thinks *look eight*.

Audra's hand lifts a bell, but there is no need. Already a man is stepping from the shadows, acquiring definition. His grey hair has fled his head except for round the ears. His name is Jenkins, he has served Audra's family since he was twenty, and as he extends his arm, tilts the bottle, details glug out with the thick Bordeaux. *Like a fountain*, thinks Jenkins, then lifts his arm. He once killed a man. That man was Daniel Caldwell, and he had it coming, but there was so much blood. As Jenkins steps back, returns to shadow, he recalls that look on Caldwell's face, as if he knew some—

'Oh,' says Maude, but so quietly the others pay no mind. A red stain of her creation crawls next to her fork. It must be stopped. But it cannot be stopped. She pushes her side plate over the blemish but it is no good. The others will·see her mistake even through the plate. They will not need to confer. The verdict has been known for years. All that remains is for it to be delivered. 'You are no longer our friend,' they will say in unison. And Maude will accept this judgement. Because she has always been an impostor: not as pretty as Elizabeth, as stylish as Audra, cleverer than both, too clever for the men. She says what she knows is true with no thought for whether this might be welcome. She talks as she writes, or she writes as she talks, perhaps it is all the same. Words appear in her mind, on her tongue, dropping down a silken thread until a pattern is formed, spoken, traced in ink, forming a web for spiders, flies, the constellation of—

And once again there is shouting. In the dark of the street a whistle is blown repeatedly. Turning quickly you see a white dog streak by, its thoughts of steak, the pain in its paw, and then there is a confusion of shadows. Names and thoughts un-joined to faces in the London dark. It might be easier to sink beneath these waves, to surrender to knowing and not knowing, to live only in gloom. But you cannot resist that well-lit room where things seem definite. Flat knives tap crystal as the main course enters. A mock hush descends. Six pairs of eyes watch Reggie rising (there, look number nine).

'Dear friends, it is my honour to once again welcome our friend the flounder.'

'Hello flat face!'

'Linus, that's not nice!'

'Oh, do you think it can *hear*? Should I *apologise*?'

You can't tell what the servants make of this exchange – all stand near the far wall, in the background, where the light is weaker. In shadow they watch fish and new potatoes, and only when a woman with red hair comes forwards into the light do you understand that what she, Maisie, finds most strange is that these toffs think it normal for their plates to fill with food, for them to scoff it up and then get more. As if it was all bloomin' magic. Like we're their mums and dads and them just big children. They wouldn't know work if it bit their arse, and the pity, the *shame*, is that the war didn't kill more of them.

But that's just Maisie, and it can't be easy, what with her mother and that leg (and is it the right or left?). Lucy, the girl nearest to her, would probably know, unless of course this is Gwen. Next to her is Sue, who has a mole, or a birthmark, and Jenkins, who is furthest in shadow, now seems barely present.

And while you fumbled in shadows Something has Occurred. Reggie, who is still standing, has brought his hand to his throat. Though he has been adrift so long, now a signal has flashed. Either he speaks to Audra or goes quietly home, climbs the stairs to the attic, unfolds the oilcloth, lifts the revolver and then—

The scream is a long rip in the dark. It is a pillar of flame. Turn and run and your light can race down alleyways, passages, perhaps into a home where chalk-faced children cough even in dreams. You can follow the scream or you can stay with your face to the glass. Even if the streets were bright with bleaching light – even if it were Day – the choice would need to be made. Because you will never be a light that burns brightly enough. You and I are candles. We gutter, we drip. We differ in our burning times, not in the light we cast.

New Traffic Patterns
May Emerge

Sally is a worried tiger because they are late. Her mother drives round the block and when they return Sally spies the perfect space – right outside the old church hall – but they cannot stop. When they come round again a dirty white van has taken the space, and this seems unfair, it was *theirs*. But then a parked car eases out and everything is fine.

*

Injuries, break ups, deaths of friends: these were normal, awful life events that Chris could have managed. If they'd happened over several years he might have coped. But it had been a year of four funerals and a poisoned cat. His flat had been burgled; his car stolen; he'd been punched in the face by a stranger. His perfect girlfriend Rachael had tried to stab him, then broken up with him by text.

He had never cried as much, been so unable to sleep, and yet he was not depressed. He sometimes wished he were.

There were pills for that, and therapy, the notion of a path that wound back to health. What he felt seemed permanent.

*

When Sally bursts through the double doors a tall girl squeals her name. All heads turn; they gather round; her tiger make up is praised.

'I'll see you later,' her mother says. 'Mrs Gray will bring you home.'

The sea of children parts for the birthday boy. Lucas is wearing black jeans and a blue shirt with a green wool tie. On his head an orange paper crown has slightly split. Before Sally can say, 'Happy Birthday' he has launched into the breathless, delighted speech only she evokes.

'It's the last one I saved it for you it's like mine do you like it?'

She takes the hat. She'd prefer green. 'It's lovely,' she says.

Lucas bows and offers her his arm, and in this childish, gallant way, the party begins. Fifty years later, as he walks through an airport, one of the huge lights will drop from the ceiling and miss him by only a foot.

'You look beautiful,' he says and then the music starts. Sally can't see where it's coming from, knows only that it's getting louder and keeps changing its mind.

*

The traffic is bad: the bus lurches; there is no momentum. But Chris is in no hurry. Being on the bus is no worse than being at work. In both he only watches things appear and vanish. At work these are mostly words on a screen, and though it is his hand that cuts and pastes, he is not involved.

He sees broken glass, a damaged car, policemen standing still. Then the traffic starts to flow. When he arrives at the offices of Conflict Resolution he is barely late. It is a small office of only six people, and yet only Adam answers when he says, 'Good morning'. He sits down and turns on his computer and soon the moving begins. He fixes bad text, but more arrives, as it always will.

'Did you see the Botswana piece?' says Adam. '*That* was a war crime. He used about ten commas per sentence.'

Chris nods and Adam makes a sound of disgust. For the next half an hour no one in the office speaks. They click and type and maybe, in some small way, help to resolve conflict. Chris really has no idea. What was a passion is now a job he watches himself do. Even poor, jaded Adam is more engaged than that. After his kidnap, torture and then escape, he'll do his job much better.

*

Sally holds Lucas's small, damp hand as she sits on the wooden floor. They eat crisps and baby sausages wrapped in bacon. They eat cheese and pineapple on sticks. There is trifle, blancmange, three kinds of ice cream, green jelly with mandarin pieces suspended like fish. As they eat an old man plays the accordion. Sally doesn't want the song to end. She wants to sit with Lucas till their hair is white.

But the song is changing, slowing down, becoming one she knows. With every note, the end comes closer, till there are the words. *Hap-py birth-day dear Lu-cas. Happy birthday to you.*

With that, the old man takes a bow. The children clap and cheer except for Neil Gray whose nose bleeds a lot because he picks it. He'll continue this bad habit well into his twenties, right until he loses an arm climbing Ben Nevis.

*

There is a fifty-pound note on the back seat of the bus. It is not folded or crumpled, has not come from a pocket, it is cash-machine crisp. It looks to have been placed quite deliberately. Obviously not for him: it is one of those self-aggrandising acts of kindness that mean nothing because they are random. Fifty pounds will not change his life, or Rachael's mind, will not bring back the dead. But it is just as easy to take it as not, so Chris puts it in his pocket and sits down. He looks at the traffic, its stop and start. When he was in America with Rachael they saw a sign by the highway that said *New Traffic Patterns May Emerge.* They didn't know what it meant, and so it seemed funny.

He is almost home when he remembers he has nothing

for dinner. He goes into the Bamboo Palace take away and orders three dishes. Liu Jianqing says thank you then goes into the kitchen to give the order to his brother Liu Xiaoguo. He comes back out, says, 'Fifteen minutes' then smiles in a way that seems apologetic. As if having to wait any length of time is unreasonable. As if he and Chris are friends despite knowing nothing about him except his liking for fried tofu. Jianqing asks him for money in the same sheepish manner, and at first Chris is about to hand over the fifty pound note, but then offers his debit card.

Later, at home, he will take the note from his wallet and stick it to the wall by his bed. He will look at it in the half-darkness as Xiaoguo and Jianqing clean the kitchen, count the takings, speak of their mother's health. She has a lump in her breast, and they are so worried. But the tests will be negative.

*

At most birthday parties the old man and his accordion would have been the climax. But Lucas's father has big hands covered in rings. He owns nine restaurants and drives a long grey car. They live in a mansion with a swimming pool. No son of his will have an ordinary party.

The food is quickly cleared away. Cages are brought in. There are six of them, too large for hamsters, each shrouded in cloth. They wait on tables while sawdust is scattered, fences erected, expectation built. Sally puts her lips to Lucas's ear, whispers, *Tell me, what is it?*

'That tickles!' he says then rubs his ear and one day they'll get married. They'll stand on a big white cake and she'll—

Baby rabbits. Grey, with neatly folded ears, or just *black*. A darkness in the shape of a bunny.

The children crowd round the enclosures. They listen to a woman in blue overalls explain how to pick up a rabbit properly. First she strokes its back, then ears, then slides her hand under it. 'You have to be gentle,' she says.

Lucas goes first, as is only proper. He picks up a black one without any problem, but puts it down quickly. 'It's very warm,' he says.

Juliet goes next because she has a chinchilla and two gerbils at home. She wants so much to be a vet, but although she'll try her hardest, she'll never succeed.

It is Sally's turn.

*

Reluctantly, he opens his eyes, and then the light is inside. It is the sun of the first day of June and it pushes through his brain, from the retina, along bundled pathways, all the way to the back. It is a neural detonation. It is a leap of flame.

He sees the bank note. He showers. The water is so hot and forceful that after a few minutes he sits down. He closes his eyes, tries to retreat, but the summer light is still jumping about in his head like a demented spark.

The bus is slow and he has to stand. A pushchair keeps jabbing his leg. The father could fold it, the girl could stand, be carried, but no, despite the looks, the sighs, the man remains defiant. There is no way to escape. He is surrounded, pressed against people, and though some of them will not outlive their parents, this doesn't empty the bus.

When the doors next open a warm breeze enters the bus and then without intention or even choice he is saying, *Excuse me, excuse me*, and then just pushing through. He is on the street and moving north. The pavement is crowded but at no point are there obstacles during the next half hour. Sometimes he must slow, be patient, but even then he isn't stopped. He is a long fuse burning down.

The spark of him reaches the office. He passes Craig, his boss – who will win £10,000 in next week's lottery – then goes to his desk. He turns on his computer, opens his email, and there, amidst the war and rape, is the shock of Rachael's name.

*

Sally is sure the rabbit will bite. Teeth will puncture her finger like the stapler that went into Ivan's. Two tiny holes, then blood.

The rabbit sniffs her hand. Its whiskers do not tickle. They are like a scrape of velvet. Her hand trembles. The rabbit opens its mouth. Then her hand is smoothing its ears. They are almost as long as its body; every time she strokes them down they stand up again. Sally strokes the ears of the rabbit that doesn't bite, and never will, and although it is definitely someone else's turn, Sally cannot stop .

*

It is a terrible, wonderful message.

Hi Chris, hope you're ok. It's been so long since we talked. Can we meet tomorrow?

Even for Rachael, it's brief: she has always written in tweets.

The message is either completely straightforward or totally opaque. She just wants to talk, a perfectly reasonable request but for the fact that nothing between them was reasonable during the final week. Will she now explain why she broke his car windows and put the glass in his shoes? Why her keys were wedged between her fingers as she ran at him?

He can't think while sat at the computer. He goes outside, passing Sue on the stairs, and if she doesn't respond to his nod it's because her back is giving her trouble, except that the problem isn't her back. It's the growth of something she can't feel, will never see, but maybe has an inkling of, just as Chris has a suspicion that he is in the early stages of being infected with something as dreaded.

He goes outside and walks. Through the streets, into parks, along the river, pausing only when traffic or construction allow no other choice. The smart thing is not to meet. Even if she finds him – he's moved since they broke up – she will only scream and throw whatever's to hand. However embarrassing or painful, it will only be one wound. Not that fearful checking of every moment they are together. Someone that has hurt you badly never forgets how.

But the simple, smart decision resists being made. Every indisputable reason has an answering image. Yes, she is crazy, but not always. Not when she slept on the deck of the houseboat as the water tugged them along so surely there was no need for an engine, or worry, only a corkscrew and contraception.

Not when she baked him twenty-nine cakes with candles.

Yes when she slapped a girl who said he was boring. But that time, he liked it.

By the time Chris gets back to the office, the diagnosis is clear. He has contracted hope.

*

Time is up, the rabbits are caged. It's the end of the party, the return of homework, not enough TV. Only Lucas seems unconcerned.

'Thank you for coming,' he says to each of them as parents start to appear. He shakes the boys' hands, kisses girls on the cheek, but Sally is not jealous. Once everyone but Neil Gray has gone (he sits on his own, picking his nose) Lucas takes her hand. 'Did you like the party?' he says with great concern.

She nods.

'What was your favourite?'

'You know.'

'They were lovely. We're keeping two.'

'Can I visit them?'

'Of course.'

'When?'

'Tomorrow.'

Sally throws her arms round him, and they hug, until he gives her a squeeze that makes her yelp. He lets go and they giggle. Mrs Gray is here.

'Look at you two,' she says. 'I thought this was a birthday not a wedding. You stop that,' she says to Neil. 'You know what'll happen.'

Guiltily, he removes his finger.

'Are you ready Sally?'

'Yes Mrs Gray,' she says and stands. Lucas looks hurt, almost close to tears, until she says, 'See you tomorrow.' He recovers enough to smile and wave and then her shoes are going clip clop on the floor like hooves. They turn corners, are out the door when Mrs Gray says, 'Oh no. What did I tell you?' Her voice shifts to anger. 'I *told* you Neil, and you still did it. Why?'

Neil's blood drops from his nose, to the ground, onto his sleeve, his fingers, then he is pinching his nose. 'Sobby,' he says, and his mother takes his other hand.

'Sally, stay here a minute. We won't be long, I promise.'

Mrs Gray and Neil go back inside, leaving Sally with her piece of birthday cake wrapped in a damp napkin. She looks at the drops of blood, and after a moment, smears one with her shoe. She doesn't look up when a car door shuts, nor when footsteps approach.

'All on your own?' says a man and she hesitates because she does not talk to strangers. Except that he is not. 'Mrs Gray is coming back,' she tells the man who brought the rabbits.

*

Chris is good at reading faces: Rachael's has a new chapter. It has been written by her, on her, during their time apart. The crow's feet of her eyes spread further; her lips lack blood. Things have happened in her plot that she did not expect. Otherwise she wouldn't be eating lunch with him at this French place where the tablecloths are viciously white, the cutlery too large. She has picked this place because it is safe ground: she can cook most of the things on the menu; her French is so good that when she speaks to the waiter he doesn't reply in English.

But she isn't eating. She is talking about people he doesn't know, her trip to Chile, her recurring problems with her phone, everything but the fact that they used to fuck and be in love and once she tried to stab him. They could just be old friends catching up.

He eats and sprinkles words on hers and he has been so stupid. He'd prefer it if she'd lunge at him with this dagger of a fork. At least that would be clear. He'd go to hospital, get bandaged, wring the neck of hope.

'Are you seeing anyone?' she asks then takes a sip of water.

'No,' he says, and her only reaction is to dab her lips with a napkin. And it would definitely be wrong, and weak, to ask her the same question.

'What about you?' he says and her response is swift. The corners of her mouth twitch up with what must be contempt. She takes another sip, looks at him, says, 'There's been no one since you.'

'Really?'

'Yes.' Her voice gains volume. 'Apart from some people I fucked.'

The restaurant does not go quiet. The other diners keep speaking, they are not bothered, all except a man sitting on his own who has not had sex for eleven years. He will eat two desserts, have coffee, then take a leisurely walk to Waterloo Bridge which he will then leap off.

Chris needs a moment before he accepts what Rachael means. What had been a flickering idea is now almost steady.

She doesn't want dessert or coffee. She seems nervous, in a hurry, when she asks for the bill.

When it arrives he pulls out his wallet; curtly she says, 'Don't'. As if he were reaching for a gun and she the quicker draw.

They walk to the corner, where she stops.

'I have to go to Vauxhall,' she says.

Not *this was lovely. Or good to see you.* And the light flickers once more.

As for what happens next, if he were looking at the people around he'd see their alarm. Heads are turned, mouths taken from phones; hers is a savage attack. For those first few seconds it isn't a kiss, more a mutual hurt. She is biting his lip and his teeth get bashed and he is sure he tastes blood. Then he is able to open his mouth. And her tongue is less of a weapon. Admittedly, for a moment he cannot breathe, but then their tongues are turning circles, establishing orbit.

She is the one who breaks the circuit. Closes it again. They kiss and for that instant nobody has died. No cat has been poisoned, no flat burgled; love is apparently possible again.

Rachael removes her mouth and looks at him. He is smiling, but she is not. Her gaze interrogates.

'Chris,' she says. 'I'll call tonight. I'll explain.'

With that she is a back that weaves between people, crosses the street, descends underground.

He looks at his phone. 3 p.m. He won't go back to work.

*

The rabbits' faces press against the bars. The van smells of them, of paint.

*

In a playground children spin while a giant mouse keeps time.

A tall clear pipe traps a ball it fires into the air. Three or four storeys, rising, falling, endlessly propelled. Straining up towards the sky and never reaching it.

There are buildings too old to be standing.

And there is John Bunyan, who across centuries, and via stone, speaks of sleep and dream. The statue is on the corner of a building that evades attention. Its heavy wooden door is closed, and there is no number, no name.

Chris isn't stopped by red lights or men or cars that kill pedestrians, cyclists, several times a week. He walks as if pulled by horizontal gravity. The only thing that slows him comes from people's mouths. They speak of bitches, wankers, shits, having fucking had enough. They say this to their phones, their friends, themselves, and though this doesn't stop him – he is too happy – it is a source of friction.

And so there is a fumbling for earphones. There is Brahms. For the next few minutes Chris walks with no more effort than it takes to fall. Then a siren wails, then another – scaffolding has collapsed onto four Spanish tourists – but the volume can go up. Although he sees the ambulance, then the fire engines, they are like a section of the orchestra coming in too late. It is regrettable, certainly awful, but ultimately no competition for Rachael, perhaps already in Vauxhall. Rachael who is not to be trusted, only to be loved.

Between buildings a flash of river acts as invitation. He turns to it, and the music swells, and as he reaches the bridge two police cars appear. Their sirens shatter his thoughts of her and for a hateful second he remembers holding the leather strap of his father's coffin, the strap of his best friend's. He is on the ground and bleeding, lying on a stretcher.

But the sirens pass and the view expands; first the Southbank, then the Festival Theatre, and soon there is a panorama that demands attention. There is no room for his past and who the fuck wants it? He only exists in the present.

Over the river, striking south, through the afternoon. Heading home, but in roundabout fashion, because evening, when she will call, is three, four hours away. The sun is still high, not that it matters, because here the buildings are low. Take away the cars, the roads, and this is almost a village, that place where people's cares were limited to hunger, disease, invasion, the attentions of wolves. In the present, with the lack of these, the place seems benign. Slow traffic and leafy streets and nine types of recycling bin. Rachael, if transplanted here, might be a different person.

That it could be so simple. It might not be, but then again – it's not impossible. She hates crowds and has always said pollution gives her a headache. Here, between the silver birches, she might acquire peace.

He starts to pay attention to the 'For Sale' signs. He can't afford them, but they could. She and he could live happily ever after in one of these mock-Tudor castles. It could be their child (or even children) playing in this injury-proof playground. They could be the ones climbing, swinging, flying down the slide's silver tongue. There must be twenty, thirty kids in this playground, all of them seeking, most of them finding, their own kind of fun. Two of these will die in a fire; one will commit murder.

He reaches a crossroads. The traffic is thickening into rush hour. For the first time since he started walking he isn't sure which way to go. All the roads are unappealing: grey, busy, lined with warehouses or an empty lot. He'll have to take one to get home, to receive her call – she hates talking on mobiles – and what did she mean by 'evening'? Most people would think this meant eight or nine o'clock; but if she decides it means six, he'll miss her call. Something most people wouldn't mind – they'd call back at seven, or eight, or nine – but then most people don't try and stab the person they claim to love.

*

Sally tries to stand, but fails. She tries again. She fails.

*

Cars pass in a metal line. Although she said 'I'll explain,' he doesn't see how she can. There are no reasons left. He knows her parents split up when she was nine; that she had an abortion when she was fifteen. At seventeen she ran away for three months with a much older man. He knows about the self-harm, the medication, the shoplifting. Each has been invoked as cause, as deserving of pardon. The only trauma yet to be invoked is some secret fatal disease, or, failing that, abuse. And how much does that explain, let alone excuse?

The evening will be warm: he won't miss having a jacket or sweater at eight or nine or ten. He'll walk and the phone will ring and so what if the light of hope goes out. Even before her message things were getting better. Admittedly, he wasn't happy, but he'd certainly felt worse. The best thing for him is to stay away from her.

The street curves, and he follows it, and suddenly he's tired. Everything around is dirty, the walls, the pavement, the mini cab office. The menu in Southern Fried Chicken has been sun-bleached white. It is one of those rare parts of London that can't be gentrified.

He walks on, and as the road widens, the pavement starts to narrow. He's closer to the passing cars, which are, or seem to be, going much faster, and this makes him angry. Why the fuck should he be in danger? All it needs is a trip, slip, the push of a stranger, and he will be dead.

As if on cue, three men appear, two of them white, one black. They are young and holding beer bottles and laughing very loudly. As they near, they fall silent. The pavement isn't wide enough for the four of them.

He's about to step aside, but the black one does first. The space he opens is not on either side of the group; it is in the middle.

They are looking at him, not talking. His heart punches his chest.

As he steps closer, the gap seems to narrow, but there is no good response. When he goes through, they'll attack. If he looks scared, or tries to run, they'll do the same.

He walks towards the gap. They will use their fists, their feet, the bottles.

One of the white men raises his arm; and yet Chris passes through.

He walks on, heart still hurting, till he reaches a junction. There he sits on a wall and closes his eyes and the darkness is kind for a while. He can see and think nothing as he quietly cries.

The sound of horns retrieves him. He opens his eyes and sees a queue of vehicles on the near side of the road. The closest is a white van so dirty no rain will trouble its filth.

The van moves forward enough for him to see its rear doors. Their windows are just as dirty, which is why he doesn't notice the face at first. Small and mostly orange with black lines spreading from its mouth. *Make up*, he thinks, and the van moves forward, and though it is clearly a child he can't decide on the sex. As if to help him, a hand rubs the window, but it makes little difference. *A girl*, he thinks, but it's mostly a guess, though really, what does it matter? He would just as soon wave back to a little girl or boy, especially one waving so enthusiastically. He isn't sentimental about children – they're not innocent or angels – but neither is he indifferent. This little girl with her cute make up is exactly what he needs to see. Something so unambiguously joyous puts things in perspective.

The cars are moving faster but there is still time. Time to

see her bang on the glass and – such is her excitement – shout something he can't hear. Perhaps it isn't even words, just her little roar.

And even as her face recedes, he's reaching for his phone. He'll call Rachael and she'll answer. From now on things are going to be fine.

The Ballad of Poor Lucy Miller

Every morning, except Sunday, Lucy Miller catches the 8 o'clock bus. She dismounts at Paddington, walks down the cobbled street, revolves through the door of Galtons, moves through Perfumes, then through Linens, ascends to the mezzanine which principally sells gloves.

Sometimes she is tired, exhausted, and sometimes the customers are rude, but even when a woman puts a pin in Lucy's wrist, even as the red bead swells, even then the onlookers will see Lucy smile. And when the great clock chimes six times, when the clothed hands float their way out, Lucy puts on her coat and turns through the brass doors. She walks down the cobbled street and pulls her thin coat tight. The wind is from an icy place where even vicious bears feel sorry for poor Lucy. She is small, and without fur. Her brain has a tumour. It is pressing on the nerves that make her sense of smell. The only thing she smells is violets, just after she wakes.

Lucy waits at the bus stop. She knows something is wrong with her. Last week the doctor made her breathe through a cardboard tube into a clock-like device whose hands moved not that much. He told her to take off her skirt and pants and then said, 'Lie down, please.' Then he said, 'Please stay still' and shone a small light into her anus. When, after thirty seconds – during which neither spoke – Lucy twitched and tried to turn over, the good doctor said, quite sternly, 'I told you, lie *still.*'

The windows are the colour of butter; it begins to rain. Lucy has no umbrella and so is quickly drenched. In her sodden state, with the rain running down her face, several people think she is crying.

The bus is crowded; Lucy must stand and sway next to a woman with sharp elbows.

When Lucy gets off the bus it has at least stopped raining. She crosses the bridge, climbs up the hill, walks down her road where the streetlights are out. She looks in the windows, whose curtains are closed, but there is still a yellow line that speaks of snug parlours, waiting meals, fires prepared to welcome. She walks and gradually, house by house, she conjures the father, the mother, the daughter, their faces flushed, the love and kindness in their eyes, and something runs in front of her and almost makes her fall. She stops and gasps and the darkness shifts with an evil swish of a tail.

Lucy tries to collect herself. She looks up, in hope of stars, but above, always clouds.

She makes her key bite through the lock. 'Mother, I'm home,' she calls out, and then a hand-bell rings. Lucy takes off her wet coat and the bell rings again. She sighs and climbs the leaning stairs that she fell down last month.

Her mother is propped up in bed. She is wearing a hat and gloves, and even though she sees Lucy she rings the bell again.

'Where were you?'

'I'm sorry, the bus was late.'

'Sorry never helped a horse.' Her mother opens her mouth and points at her brown teeth. 'They're hungry. Almost dead. *I'm* almost dead. Then you can have all the butcher's boys you want.'

Poor, poor Lucy Miller has never even been *touched*. Not by a clerk from Smith & Hyde, not by a butcher's boy.

'Mother, I'm sorry. I'll get your tea.'

'Don't want it.'

'Please, Mother.'

'Please yourself. That's what you do my girl.'

Lucy goes downstairs. She sits at the kitchen table and gives her head to her hands. Her father was killed by a single brick that fell from their chimney. Her mother never speaks of him except when she's asleep.

The bell rings and rings and rings and her hands hold her head.

'Something with a bit of blood,' her mother says and laughs.

*

Lucy smells the ghost of violets in the near dawn. She wishes that her room were full of clean chrysanthemums. There is a flower stall on the way to the bus stop. One day she will stop and buy some. Even if she cannot smell them, she will see their heads, their stems, the petals they hold tight.

The charcoal light is smudged to grey when she slides from the bed. She puts on her worn dressing gown and goes into the bathroom. The water in the toilet is an intense yellow. It reminds her of the fields of rape she ran through as a child. Her dress and legs were stained with pollen but she did not fall.

Lucy flushes the toilet and turns on the tap. The basin fills. She thinks of Sunday. The day that she is free.

*

On Saturday she sees at least a hundred hands. Long ones, small ones, pale ones, red ones, clean ones, ones with brown stains under their chipped nails. It is as if the town has become ashamed of its hands. *Cover me*, the fingers say, as they rest on glass, linen, leather, wool, her flesh. The current hands are rooster's claws, old and slimy and grasping. They rest on hers while the gentleman looks in her eyes and talks about stitching. There used to be two rows on the fingers but now there are only one and did she know why, hmm? 'Spaniards,' he says as his wife comes over and then he lifts his hands. He says, 'I need a pair for the Opera, my old ones are quite worn.' Lucy flushes and feels like a bird in a cage that has been thrown out of a high, high window. The bird can fly, it knows it can, but it is in the cage and falling and here, oh dear, is the ground.

She stands and helps them hide their fingers. Her father never hid his hands. Whenever he fixed, or painted, or mended, his hands could always be seen.

She doesn't like her Sunday gloves. But it's the only way.

*

Is it autumn, is it winter, no one seems to know. Although the leaves are mostly off the trees the sun is working hard. Flies bounce at windowpanes; women on their way to church doubt their heavy coats. And Lucy, when she wakes finds a bright rectangle of light on the wall by her head. In the clean shape of its goodness she sees many things. She stares at it and smells the violets until she is summoned.

'You stink of meat,' her mother says, but it does not matter. Lucy feeds her, Lucy wipes her, Lucy reads from Psalms to her till Mrs Richards comes. Mrs Richards, lean and grey, has always lived next door. Mrs Richards will sit with her mother from eleven to six.

Lucy scrapes a tin of pilchards into a small pot. She puts the pot in a bag, the bag in her pocket. Then she takes her thick gloves from the drawer and puts them in her coat. She says goodbye to Mrs Richards then goes out the back door. She walks to the back of the garden then opens the small gate. She steps into the dim alley that cuts between the houses. She walks down it, her footfalls loud, and it is like a long dark gullet with a mind to swallow. It must smell of decay and urine but it widens like a cinema screen and there is the canal— silver, blue, a line that flows and stretches. The water contains the sky and poor, poor Lucy Miller feels herself relax. Her neck and head still have a tightness, her ears expect the bell, but as she wanders by the water she begins to smile. The sun is warm. She is free. There is enough time.

She walks until there are no houses, just the gasworks and the biscuit factory. Lucy sits on a metal bench that the paint has flecked off. She takes the bag from her pocket, removes the jar, then places it on the ground. Next she takes the gloves from her pocket and puts them beside her. She stares at the water. Waits.

The sun shines and shines and shines on Lucy's excellent skin. A woman with a green scarf pushes a pram past. She calls to Lucy. 'Beautiful day!'

'Yes it is!' she replies.

Two boys pass on shiny bikes the red of fire engines. They streak by without a look and something in their ease and grace impresses Lucy deeply.

Two o'clock. Three o'clock. And then, although she hears nothing, she turns to the left. A small black cat is looking at the pot. She looks at his tail, his paws, and her scalp begins to itch, but in a pleasant way. It is like her skin is sighing through small mouths. They are breathing out the week, not all of it, by any means, but Monday (when her mother hit her), and some of Tuesday, too.

She picks up the pot and takes a fish from it. She dangles it by its oily tail and the cat comes nearer. Its tiny face is soft and eager; it is not much more than a kitten and if a passing painter saw this scene he would find it so charming, so delightful, he'd have to stop and do the beauty of it justice. It would be touching, it would be heartfelt; it would sell a million boxes of chocolate.

Lucy watches the cat sniff closer. She drops the fish and then the cat begins to quickly eat. She looks at the water, the sun, the cat and things seem so composed, so ready, the itch spreads down her neck like a line of red ants.

As Lucy reaches for the gloves, the pain of Wednesday leaves. The gloves are thick and darkly stained, her fingers small in them. As if these were adult gloves and she only a child.

The cat finishes the fish. It looks at her. It licks its lips. 'Alright,' she says and drops a fish the cat pounces on. She wonders if it has a name; if it lives nearby.

Lucy leans and grasps its neck and squeezes very hard. The cat makes a choking sound and scratches at the gloves. Lucy grabs one of its back legs and pulls it toward her. The cat screams like a scalded baby; she puts her foot on it. She presses down on its small skull and Thursday, Friday shift.

Lucy raises her heel and the cat does not move. Although the animal is breathing, it has given up.

She lifts it gently from the ground; the cat has lost an eye. Its breath wheezes out, then in, and she is free of Saturday, that longest day of hands. She is glad, she is relieved, but there is still a weight. It feels large, and like a stone, and it is in her head, her stomach; it seems firmly lodged.

Lucy takes the twitching creature to the canal's edge. She holds the cat's head under till the bubbles stop.

*

Next day the golden hands on Galtons' clock tell Lucy she is late. The pretty girls in Perfumes smirk; the ladies in Linens laugh. Lucy Miller is *late*, they say, and giggle at her blush.

She climbs to the mezzanine. 'Twenty-four minutes,' says Mr Mackie. 'Twenty-four minutes. Because you were sleeping. It must not happen again.'

'Yes, Mr Mackie.'

He frowns. 'I want you to clean the storeroom. Do not kill the spiders.'

*

Lucy seldom goes to the park during her lunch break. There and back is half the time of which there's not enough. But Tuesday is clear and sharp; the colours all say Yes. She sits on a bench and eats. Dogs are playing in the leaves. A tramp is fast asleep.

She can barely taste her sandwich. If the cheese were yellow shit, she probably wouldn't know.

But the leaves are coming down: orange, yellow, red. They

seem weightless as they fall; as if they could float back up whenever they so chose.

The tramp sleeps on; the dogs roll over; she breathes slowly out.

*

Next morning she wakes without hearing the bell. Lucy looks in on her mother; she is fast asleep. Lucy thinks about a long-lost Sunday when they had a picnic. Her father drove them to the Downs. Their sandwiches had tongue. They stood together on the hilltop while chaffinches flew round.

Her mother has not been outside for almost seven years.

*

Mr Mackie has broken his leg. Eight to ten weeks, says Mr Walker, a dusty man whose left hand shakes because he's frightened of people.

Lucy looks at the gloves on the counter. Rows of white and rows of brown. A single row of green. The largest gloves are close to her, the child's ones far away.

Lucy watches the hands of the clock that shine and grudgingly move.

A mother and her girls come in. The girls are painted wooden dolls that can't stand on their own. Their hands are shaped from porcelain; they'll never have to work.

As Lucy clothes the girls' pale hands, they stare at her and whisper. She shrouds their gloves in tissue paper. They go in a box.

*

The carpet in the park is thick; the hands above are bare. Lucy sits on the same bench and opens her bag. She removes a small hard apple. She inspects it, then takes a bite. She enjoys the texture.

A blur of movement in the bushes: the tramp from before. He has a full, brown beard and string around his trousers. He stops and stares at her then moves behind a tree.

Lucy finishes her apple. Then she eats the core. The pips are yielding in her mouth as she scans the leaves. Their colours are not in rows: they each chose their place. She thinks of woods, the tall dense trees. Their leaves piled like rugs.

Her father used to catch her when she flew down the slope. Arms out but no plane noise because she was a girl. Down and down, her legs too fast, then crash into his arms.

By next weekend it will have rained. The carpet will be soiled. She will go on Sunday. Leave her gloves at home. The tram to Epsom, then a bus; then the time between the trunks where bells can never ring.

'For you,' a hoarse voice says. The tramp looks like Karl Marx. He extends his palm which holds a red oak leaf. 'For you,' he says and then comes closer. There is something on the leaf. It is wet, but not like water; there are some white lumps.

He looks down and her eyes follow. His penis is small and brown and in his other hand. When Lucy tries to stand the tramp pushes her back. 'For you,' he says and then she feels the leaf against her face.

She screams but when she tries to stand he hits her in the eye.

'For you,' he says and then she hears the police whistle blast.

*

On Thursday she goes to the doctor. He examines her.

*

When Lucy wakes on Friday morning she cannot smell violets. The tumour has grown so large it has killed the nerve.

She pulls the blanket over her head. Soon, the bell will ring. She wonders when will this end. Her mother, although insane, could live for many years. She could stand among the gloves till she is grey and small.

She does not want to get married. This means fetching, carrying, men putting things in her. Mary from soft furnishings can talk of nothing else. She says it hurts too much unless they're in the bath.

Lucy raises the blanket and looks at the clock. Six-thirty. She should get up.

The toilet contains large black pellets, like the droppings

of sheep. She flushes the toilet and moves to the basin and then the bell begins to ring like it's the end of the world.

'Where were you? With the meat?'

'Mother, I came right away.'

'Liar. Eating sausages. He will get you fat.'

There are three more black pellets on the bedside table. Her mother points to them. 'Good meat.' She takes one between thumb and finger. She opens her mouth.

Lucy moves and shouts, too late. She can feel the week in her, like fifty pounds of lead. It will slowly sink from her head, through her neck, her belly, till it tears through her feet.

*

On Saturday Lucy buys a large tin of sardines.

On Sunday she cannot wait for good old Mrs Richards. Her coat is already on. The gloves are in her pocket.

Her mother's bell is quiet because she's eating tripe. The only bells are those outside but they can be ignored.

Lucy puts her hand to her cheek. She thinks about the leaves.

Finally, at ten past eleven, she hears a frail knock. Lucy admits Mrs Richards who must leave at two.

Through the back gate, down the alley, Lucy almost runs. The sky is a sheet of metal being lowered on ropes. If it rains, she has no chance: the cats will not come out. The week will stay in her.

As she reaches the canal she feels the first spot. Dumbly,

she extends her palm. Another raindrop falls. When she tilts her face up water strikes her chin. She stands there – palm out, face up – waiting, hoping, and although there is no mercy, no more rain drops fall.

She hurries on. She passes no one. When she rounds the bend, she stops. A small boy of five or six is sitting on her bench. His face is dirty; his hair is matted: he looks like a gypsy.

Get off my bench, she wants to say. But Lucy just walks on. She goes past the biscuit factory, then onto the lock. She stands where the water drops; she looks at her watch. In two hours she must relieve Mrs Richards. *Thank you very much*, she'll say and then, as soon as the door shuts, the bell will start to ring. It will toll throughout her week while she dresses the hands.

The week has been too bad. If she cannot lift it slightly, she will not survive.

Lucy cries for several minutes. Then she bites her lip. She walks back toward her bench and wipes her stinging eyes. The skin is tender where Karl Marx hit her, but there is no bruise.

As she rounds the corner the boy stares at her. This time she does not walk past. She stops and says, 'Hello.' The boy continues staring. 'What's your name?' she says but he does not respond. Perhaps he does not understand. Perhaps the boy is shy, or simple, or does not know English.

'I'm Lucy,' she says and smiles. 'I'm supposed to meet someone here. We'd like to sit down.' His eyes follow her hand as it moves to her pocket. They stare at the half-crown she produces. 'If you let me have the bench, I'll give this to you.' The boy stares at her outstretched palm. Neither of them moves.

Then his hand snaps out to hers and he snatches the coin. 'Thank you,' she says and steps towards him. The boy opens his mouth and spits and even as it strikes her nose he begins to laugh. His laugh is high and broken, like a fox's cry. He gets up and moves away as Lucy wipes her face. 'Get out of here,' she shouts. The boy howls out a laugh.

The boy points at Lucy as he backs away. He starts to turn, perhaps to run. And then she sees him fall. As he tilts, as his arms flail, she sees the block of wood. The gypsy boy lands on his back and she is swiftly there.

Lucy puts her boot on his chest and presses till he screams. It is the sound of something feral, something free to roam, to do whatever it pleases.

She presses down, and something gives, and days begin to lift from her, to rise like fat and glad balloons towards the sky. She raises her boot then brings it down hard and when she hears the crack of his ribs, Thursday, Friday rise.

She brings her boot down again; there is another crack. Saturday bursts from her eyes. Her foot moves to his throat.

Lucy stamps. The boy spasms. He twitches and wets himself and then lies very still. The canal hurries by. The branches call for help. As for poor, poor Lucy Miller, she has never been so happy.

Octet

The procedure is always the same: he fills in forms, he waits. After twenty or thirty minutes the first of the books arrives. Usually singly, sometimes on a trolley, until they form a tower. All morning his eyes pull in their words like a stove feeding itself. At one o'clock he goes to the canteen; by quarter past he's back. He remains in his chair until he hears the voice of a man who is never tired, does not age, who may already be dead. It is a voice he hates. *The library will be closing in fifteen minutes*, says the man. *Please return your books to the desk*. With this the tower is destroyed. He must return to the present.

He leaves the library and walks down the hill until he reaches his street. At home he eats then tries to read but usually his eyes hurt. All he can do is walk the street, slowly back and forth. He goes over the day's reading. He waits for the Thought.

On this January night the sky is clear, the moon scarcely present. He is cold and his eyes ache; his mind is a tired creature he must prod into remembering. In the morning he read about Zosimos, Fulcanelli, the learned buckles of

Paracelsus; in the afternoon it was Basilides and his Octet of Subsistent Entities. Even though that was only three hours ago he remembers only *intellect, power, verbal expression* — and what else? He concentrates and conjures *wisdom.* The other four entities are gone. What use is knowing half an Octet? This is the problem with reading. If you burn an entire forest then at least there's ash. But after fifty thousand words barely a sentence remains. No wonder he feels sick each time he turns a page.

He walks to the end of the street then stops to watch the car lights. To the right, a streak of white, to the left a smear of red. This was what those old prophets meant when they spoke of *heaven's trace, that quickened fire, paths that sear the air.* If Zosimos or Paracelsus could step through the centuries to stand by this road they wouldn't be impressed to see *carriages pulled by invisible horses.* Even then they knew they were surrounded by forces that could barely be sensed. Televisions, phones, and cars would not impress them either. Once the novelty passed they would see these things for what they were. *Applications but not answers to the only question.*

He starts back toward his house. If only he could concentrate. What he needs is a younger mind. If he'd begun at thirty, even forty, he'd have made more progress. Instead he hid himself in rooms where words built up like smoke. Everyone talking, everyone laughing, everyone so clever. They drank and danced. They found good jobs. Some of them had children. It seemed a reasonable compromise. Immortality was such a long shot. Instead of trying to make his entire self survive, surely it was better to settle for a fragment to live on after his death. Obviously, it wouldn't be him. But at least his nose, chin and laugh might move through the world. His children would point to his image, speak his name, relate incidents from his life. If they made noses and chins of their own, these might tell some of the stories, show the same pictures, but in one, perhaps two generations, his nose would vanish and then there would just be photos in an album that no living person could identify. So having children was not a partial success; the failure was simply delayed.

When he reaches the park it makes its usual promises. If he follows its paths in the dark his mental fragments will mend. This is what he did for years until last spring when the darkness suddenly moved. The pushing hands were very small. The kicks and punches were weak. He lay in the cool wet grass till the footsteps faded. Although he couldn't stand there was no need to call for help. He was warm and not uncomfortable and more or less resigned. Every life that ends has failed. His wouldn't be different. Say there really was a thought that makes a person live forever. Why should his mind be the first to think it?

At first he cannot place the scream. He has to hear it again to work out that it has come from a window on the top floor. The voice is a young woman's, maybe a girl's, screaming the word *please*. He doesn't think they're having sex. She sounds far too scared. If she screams again he'll call the police.

He puts his hands in his pockets. Waits. Maybe it's bad that she's quiet. She could be gagged, unconscious, dead. If that's the case then all that's left is her scream in his head. *Please* he hears but very quickly the word starts to shift. Now she is screaming *Peace*. That this is the fifth part of the Octet should not matter at all. He had forgotten; now he remembers. What on earth does that change?

If he were walking he wouldn't feel it. Even standing still the sensation is slight enough to dismiss. That is what most people would do. They would think it part of digestion, something caused by gas. The event is happening deep inside him, almost at his centre. It is the stage of motion before something actually moves. Like a key being twisted too gently to persuade a lock. Nothing happens. Nothing shifts. But there is potential.

After several minutes of silence a light goes on in the window. There is just time to see a man wearing a black hat with a wide brim; then the curtains are drawn.

He walks till he reaches the corner. The road he must cross is closed at one end and so does not seem like a road. Hearing nothing, he steps out, and then there is confusion. A shape pushes in front; a green light stabs his eyes. It flashes as fast as he can blink, each pulse of light a needle.

'Fuck, I nearly killed you.'

A man's voice. Angry but also scared.

'Look where you're fucking going.'

'Sorry,' he says and the cyclist mutters as he smoothes

away. His old heart is beating like an opening and clenching fist. Panicked, it wants to escape. He leans against a lamppost. He swallows and closes his eyes. Perhaps this is how he will end. Slumped in the orange pool of a streetlight fifty yards from his house. He is carrying no form of identification. He does not have a phone. When the police show the neighbours his photo, they will shake their heads.

He opens his eyes. He is alive; the world is just the same. On the pavement he can see the shadows of branches shift. There is no wind, the branches are still; and yet these shadows move. They shiver in an orange light like cracks changing their mind. Obviously, he must be wrong. There must be wind he cannot feel, tree movement he cannot see; these shadows are definitely moving.

He wets his finger, holds it up. His gaze climbs the tree. After a minute of scrutiny he looks down. On the pavement the shadows still quiver.

This is not a mistake of perception. He is not dreaming, not drunk. Something impossible is happening.

The old man stands and watches till his hands are numb. He is afraid that if he looks away the impossible will stop. He has waited most of his life for something like this moment. He could not have said what he expected. Just that it should defy the way things appear. That this is the smallest of discrepancies doesn't perturb him at all. If one impossible thing can happen, so can another.

He has three hypotheses for what is happening. The first is

that the shadow is caused by a branch, just not the branch in the present. The second is that the shadow is moving on its own. The third possibility is that it is not a shadow: it could be light that is cracked.

Without warning, fanfare or signal, the shadows cease to dance. He stares at the pavement a few more minutes, but they do not return. When he looks away and resumes walking it is without disappointment. No audience minds the curtain's fall if the play was perfect.

When he reaches his front door he is ready to go in. He is freezing and tired and tomorrow there is a tower to read. Witnessing a marvel is no reason to break the habit of decades. Not when he is on the right path.

His keys are in his hand, he is finding the correct one. Then he hears the eerie cry of the Siamese that lives next door. He does not know this cat, at least not very well. Something is wrong with its head or body because the former seems too large. It is a moody, unfriendly creature that avoids his hands. He knew the cat of the previous occupants considerably better. For years she was a simple, loving creature willing to be stroked as long as any person desired. Then there was a morning when she moved slightly away. She blinked and tilted her head to one side and then it was not like being looked at by a cat. Something else was looking out from behind her eyes. Its gaze was both an assessment and a challenge. The moment did not last long. After ten seconds of scrutiny she yawned and started washing herself. At no point in the following three weeks was there any repetition of the incident. She was the same adoring creature she had always been. He wasn't sure what to do. He was considering whether to look inside her when she disappeared.

But this cat has never seemed anything but ordinary. Even its head is not really deformed. There's no real reason it should be a certain size. Such thinking is the obstacle.

He is mildly surprised when it comes toward him, much more when it looks up and says, 'Miaow.' Not the sound but the way a human says the word. Then, more typically, it slinks away to the left. When he follows, it has gone. But there is nothing magical about its disappearance: such an act is well within its ordinary powers. The important thing is that it's given him a heading. Only in a fairy story would it lead the way.

He looks as he crosses the road that is not a road. On the other side he checks the pavement. As before, the shadows are utterly still, but now this is wrong. The wind is blowing faintly in the direction he's going. It makes no sense, and every sense. The explanation is simple. This is the wind that moved the branches that moved the shadows before. It is just as Zosimos said: *Resentment always lies between a cause and its effect. No sooner are the two uncoupled then they rush towards becoming. Both aim for the first position. Neither can give ground.* And with this thought the key in his chest engages the lock. Although it is not actually turning, neither is it separate. It is like a man in a doorway, not properly inside a room, but not outside it either. A single step, a minor twist, and the line will forever be crossed.

Just before he reaches the park a single cloud crosses the moon. Her slim shape is both veiled and seen. He has never liked her. Proud when she waxes, calm when she wanes. In no doubt that she will return.

'Shut *up*,' says a woman and laughs. Neither she or the man with his arm round her shoulders were there a moment before. They are walking so close to each other, and with such difficulty – they stagger, they weave – it seems as if they are wounded. They might as well be. They are fifty-five, maybe sixty; old enough to need the anaesthetic of each other. He doesn't blame them. It is an option he has often considered. He has been told that he is special, loved, by lips that were touching his ear. He has been offered a hand to hold until the very end. And of course he was tempted. He has made mistakes. He said words he didn't mean because they fit the moment. He got married, he had a child. He was, as the Octet says, *The Parent. Also known as The Father.*

He stands aside to let the couple pass. The woman whispers something that makes the man laugh loudly. 'You just wait,' he says. 'I call it 'Fucker's Justice'.' At this she laughs, and the man does too, and this hurts the old man. Light-headed, he leans against a wall; looks up and sees the moon uncovered. Perhaps this is all her doing: the wonders he's seen tonight could be just illusions. They might have come from dreams he has yet to have.

But even as he gasps for breath, a key within him turns. Because a word returns. *Justice, that precious thread that binds the*

Octet's parts. The thought is so vivid he closes his eyes. He feels himself moving through space. The wall is still pressing hard into his back but he is also walking forward, pushing aside the dark. He is here and also there, in the present, in the future. Everything is possible now that things are cracked. But he will have to hurry. If she can uncross a 't', undot an 'i', all sense will be lost.

Quickly, swiftly, down the street towards the waiting park. That is the place it must happen, where it nearly happened before. *For there are many wondrous things that light cannot permit.* He must stand in its quiet and dark and listen. Now the Octet is complete, a key can fully turn.

Someone is burning herbs. The smell makes him think of shrines, temples, priests intoning rituals. So many splendid beliefs; such a history of failure. Perfume the air; erect halls of marble; such theatrics make no difference if one's thoughts are wrong.

Smoke is rising from the park. He cannot see the fire. It may have happened earlier, or perhaps not yet.

He passes through the gates then walks onto the grass. The frosted ground is luminous; his footsteps are bites. He crunches his way to the place that seems darkest and there he stands, considering the stars, while the cold unwinds his scarf, unbuttons his coat, thins the sweater and shirt beneath until he feels naked. Though he tries to concentrate, *warmth* is the thought that repeats.

When the fire appears it understandably has the quality of

a mirage. At first it is only a flicker amongst the allotments at the opposite end, but then grows bright enough to illuminate a cluster of sheds. The fire is exactly what he wants, which makes him distrust it. He turns his back and thinks of the Octet but soon the flames can be heard. When a window cracks he turns and starts towards the sheds. As he nears the fire his whole body applauds. It has been a night of signs he cannot ignore, events that could have been singly imagined but not in combination. Marvels, wonders, talking creatures, a slippage in causality. Success has never been so close. But he has not won. He is still a flame that came out of the dark to which he shall return.

A siren wails. A thought begins. He looks at the fire, then up at the stars. The thought is there but not its words. He feels, he knows, the key is turning. All will be unlocked.

When this happens there is pain, no, not pain; the sensation needs a new category. Heat pulses in his head and heart. Already he is taller, stronger, neither tired nor cold. Something in him has changed.

The logic of the answer is simple. His death is like the wind that shook the branch and made the shadows move. It has already happened. First was his end, then his beginning; now he lives the constant middle.

Tomorrow he will not go to the library. Instead he is going to climb the highest hill in the city. The wind can blow; the shadows may move; he is the horizon.

Imagine that this Page is Empty

1

It is completely white.

Imagine hearing these words as you stare at a space that cannot be marked or confused.

Imagine having total focus.

Now imagine Richard.

2

Richard is 35, tall and good-looking. He has brown eyes; he is always clean-shaven; he has your father's nose. Richard is without boyfriend, girlfriend, living family or friends. He is a singular, unconnected node in a large urban setting.

At this wonderful point in human history Richard doesn't need to leave his home at all. Food, medicine, alcohol, books, toiletries, music, prostitutes and hairdressers can all be paid to arrive at his door. If Richard had enough money he'd spend weeks, months within the closed cube of his apartment on the top floor of an eroded Victorian tenement. From there his view is mostly safe. There is a rectangle of school, a square of park, diagonal lines of road. The school's beige stone recalls the walls of the children's ward where they took out his tonsils and gave him ice cream in return. This is not a bad memory. He had ice cream every day for a week. He does not know anyone who has died from tonsillitis.

The park is more problematic. From a height it reminds him of the birthday cake his mother decorated to look like a football pitch. That cake leads to other cakes, then no cakes, then far too many presents. But though this is a terrible association, it is not a surprise. After five years in that apartment the link has more form than substance. The bell it rings has been struck so often its chime is dutiful, dull.

3

White are the hallways and white are the walls, the ceilings, the grab rails, the little paper cups in the mostly white hands. White is not a good colour for a hospital. With the addition of blood, urine, pus, phlegm, accreted skin cells, pain residuals, white too easily becomes Clinical Grey, Patient Pallor, some other shade that reminds. As Richard walks the corridors to his ward he keeps his eyes down. His left hand seeks reassurance from the abrasive edge of the medicine bottle in his jacket pocket. It snuggles against his index finger, its rough arrows eager to align so the cap can come off with a Pop! like the gun he had whose cork shot ghost after ghost until the schoolyard was soaked with invisible blood.

As Richard tends the first patient of the evening – a young woman with black eye make-up and an arm wound – he thinks of the pills, safe in their bottle, doubly safe in his jacket, safer still in his locker. The arm wound is self-inflicted. It is too precise. But Richard doesn't question the young woman. Talking leads to nowhere good. He cleans the wound in silence. He tries to remain absorbed in the task but her trowel-shaped chin recalls the chin of a grey-bearded man who kept muzzled boys locked in a cellar as if they were precious wine. As Richard sutures the wound – made by a knife like the one you use for cutting tomatoes – a puff of cold dust numbs his throat. So much fear and all those boys could do was twitch and grunt in the dark. Though Richard struggles to stay in the present he is tugged towards the top of a flight of metal steps. Falling, he strikes the first step, sees Josef Fritzl, the Austrian man who kept his daughter in a cellar for 24 years during which he made her pregnant seven times. The second step is Wolfgang Priklopil, also an Austrian, who also kept a girl (though not his daughter) in a cellar for eight years. The next steps are Myra Hindley, Ian Brady, Dennis Nilsen, each name and crime another bump as he tumbles down in the dark.

The wound is closed but still he falls. 'You can go now,' he says. 'Keep the stitches dry for a few days.'

'Great. Thanks!' She seems delighted. Perhaps this has been a wonderful night for her.

Once the young woman has left the room Richard closes his eyes. The bottle is waiting, the pills are ready; but it is too soon. He is not an addict. He'll take one pill just before his break at 6 a.m. Two would be better, but then he can't work: his head and hands won't connect.

Breathing slowly, avoiding eyes, he goes to fetch the next patient. The faces don't care that there is a proper sequence, an order based on need: each of them is silently shouting that they should be next. There is hope, desire, anger, despair; each face is a set of steps. Richard can ignore the men – the patient's name is Edith – and anyone young because Edith is a name that belongs in a lavender-scented drawer lined with wrapping paper. Dried petals confetti down as he calls for her.

'Here,' says a young man (or older boy) whose hair has

been mown to the scalp. He pats a brown coat on the seat by him. 'She had to go to the toilet.'

'Are you a relative?'

'Sort of. We're neighbours.'

The young man doesn't have a regional accent. Nor does he sound posh. His voice doesn't remind Richard of someone at school, a famous person, or one of his colleagues. The voice only carries words.

4

Later, watching streaks of day, Richard tries to retrieve the young man's face. Between him and the face there is a crowd of patients and relatives he must push aside. He recalls taking blood three times. He stitched a rosy cheek. He took a moth from an eyeball; glass from a buttock; gravel from a knee. He heard a prayer not addressed to him and the brogue of the woman was enough to make him recall that a modern Western democracy still prohibits abortion. After that he fell fast. Instead of many faces there was only that of the nineteen-year-old girl who'd been brought in last month with a cross burnt onto her face with cigarette butts, probably a whole pack's worth, because it took fifteen burns to make the vertical line that ran from her forehead down her nose to the tip of her chin, and then about the same amount to go from ear to ear. This memory made him rush to the staff room, open his locker, hungrily swallow a pill. It quickly turned to smoke that billowed up from his stomach until his head was fogged. Although he still saw the girl's face, the coin-sized burns, these were only images; possibly made-up.

As Richard turns away from the window, the dawn, the brown eyes and small forehead of Edith's neighbour finally appear. He recalls the pleasingly neutral voice telling Edith that when he came to visit next day he'd bring her magazines. She was being kept in because her pulse was erratic and she seemed mildly confused. Richard could hardly look at her because she was just as much an outstretched leg as that Irish brogue. She was making him trip and tumble down thickly-carpeted stairs lined with portraits of his kind, dead grandparents. Although the stairs were softer, they hurt just as much.

Instead Richard had kept his eyes on Keith, her companion. Keith had a long face with a pointed chin; his cheeks were slightly scooped. Either his nose had been broken or it was just crooked. Keith wasn't good-looking. Nonetheless, it was a face that held his interest.

Keith could not fail to miss this degree of attention 'Is something wrong?' he asked. He rubbed the side of his mouth. 'Is there food?'

'No,' said Richard then jerked his head away. He was asking for trouble. If he'd looked any longer he'd have started to fall.

5

He will walk home; the route is mostly safe. He must pass the swimming pool, which will make him think of his mother – in the guilty way you think of yours – but he'll manage, just as you manage. He'll think of snow, of gloss.

He is at his locker when the door swings open. He doesn't want to turn but he turns. Grace has arrived for her shift. Grace is a short thirtyish woman with auburn hair. Grace is liked by everyone. She is why he works nights. In his presence she is a pillar of flame whose after-image burns his eyes. Richard doesn't know what he said or did to provoke such ardour. He has only been polite to her.

'Hello stranger!' she says. 'How was your night?'

'Busy.'

'Well, you should visit us on the day shift sometime. We're not exactly playing Scrabble!'

Her laugh is a gate opening and closing fast on her breath. She sways towards him. Although she should be starting work, Grace is in no hurry.

'You know, I've been thinking about switching to nights. That'd be much better for me. Otherwise I never get to see daylight, I just go from dark to dark.'

Again her throat opens and shuts. Her laugh belongs in a fairground. She is falling, and she loves to fall. He is the hand that pushes.

'Which means we'll be working together, won't that be great?'

'Yes. I have to go.'

She steps aside too slowly, or rather he is too fast. He brushes against her breast.

'Oops,' she says with great delight and then he's out the staffroom, down the corridor, waiting for the lift that will never arrive. The stairs spiral him round and round, making him so giddy he misses the huge letter G for Ground Floor stencilled on the wall (just as you sometimes fail to notice that one of your dear, close friends is in awful pain). He ends up in the basement where the only door is locked.

Footsteps descend. Grace has followed. Soon he will be trapped.

Her steps continue. She is is on the third floor, the second. Richard fumbles in his jacket and pulls out the medicine bottle. Swallowing the pill without water makes his throat spasm, he will surely choke, die in his own hospital. Then it's in his throat, descending, transforming into smoke. When she arrives he'll be engulfed in fluffy clouds of safety.

He waits.

A door opens.

Quiet follows.

He listens.

Nothing.

6

The barking dog remains itself; a limping man doesn't change.
All they do is bulge the curtain between him and the world.
In the pleasant haze of two pills each moment is an orphan.
Stairs do not exist. Faces are not faces: they are breath-heavy
balloons. Why shouldn't he look at the swimming pool? It is
only a home for water in which no one need drown.

7

Home, he sleeps, is running through streets, chasing, being
chased, a boy but also a man. Wise yet fleet of thought and
foot, unafraid, unhesitating, Richard runs beneath bridges,
leaps over holes, place succeeding place so quickly they are
virtually one.

Experience shouldn't be serial. If we perceive A, then B,
followed by C, it is only because our prisms split the unity
of things. Instead of white, we see colour, then colour.
Fragment; piece; shard.

8

Richard wakes in pale light that could be coming or going.
It goes. He eats dinner that is breakfast – boiled eggs, toast,
a raspberry yoghurt – then reads twenty pages from the
Memoirs of the Duc de Saint-Simon. He bought the book in a

charity shop because it was cheap and thick and the court of Louis XIV sounded removed enough from the present to be safe. The book's style is measured, dry. Though the memoirs contain many portraits of people, he is reminded of no one and nothing, not even the book itself. The pages he's already read might as well be blank.

9

People are leaving their jobs as he starts towards his. In summer he'd have to keep his eyes down, but in the winter dark the hurrying figures rarely achieve focus. Their faces light no fuse. They are a flock of muttering pigeons whose wings cannot push.

He's nearly at the hospital when something squashes underfoot. Fruit or a dropped sandwich. A hamburger. Cake. Looking down he sees a long smudge haloed by black fluid. A hot dog, no, a sock, but there are jaws, an eye. The squirrel is mostly intact.

He stops and scrapes his shoe on the kerb. Despite the hardness of the stone he still feels the squirrel's little bones break.

Then he is teetering, mentally waving his arms, struggling to maintain balance. On the step beneath the squirrel squats a crow he met twenty-five years ago. He was on the way home from school when he saw the black shuttlecock of its feathers in the gutter. Both the crow's wings were broken, but it was alive.

Falling can be mercy: every step is different. But even after twenty-five years that crow refuses to blink. Richard does not remember dead cats or dogs, beloved pets, the tragedy of Bambi's mother's death. He cannot fall further. He remains the captive of that brilliant black eye. The crow wanted something, but he didn't know what. So he did nothing. He stood and watched the bird. Passing adults saw where he was looking but didn't stop. Eventually a bus arrived with a heavy solution.

The hospital entrance is choked with a group of patients enjoying cigarettes. When a black-haired woman among them makes an anguished gasp everyone looks in her direction. She drags breath into her body, then starts to choke again. Knowing she's only laughing doesn't make the sound less awful. Her laugh follows Richard into the lift where faces demand attention. Although he tries to look past them, a voice leaps at him.

'Hi. Are you just starting work?'

Richard nods. He risks a glance. Keith raises a bag.

'I'm here to visit Edith. She needs her magazines.'

Keith's smile exposes two buck teeth his lips quickly conceal. Richard knows he is staring. Keith probably thinks he is attracted to him and that is sort of how it feels, except it isn't sexual. Keith's face requires his interest the way the fishmonger's window makes him stop. The ice-supported silver heads have nothing to say.

After seven, eight seconds of staring at Keith's face Richard's mind remains blank. The crow has gone, the squirrel too. He feels no vertigo.

'Do you mind if I come and see Edith?' he asks.

'No problem.'

And there's nothing wrong with this request: it's part of his job.

In the lift Keith chatters about Edith, how she'll be missing her cat and favourite chair and the extra strong cups of tea you could stand a spoon in. All this should remind Richard of his own grandmother, how happily she smoked, how she gasped for breath. But the strange patchwork of Keith's face keeps such thoughts at bay. The lift stops. They exit.

As they walk down the corridor leading to Edith's ward Keith seems in a hurry, as if he thinks it's a race. He gets so far ahead his face is lost from view. A wave of hot fatigue sweeps through Richard. Horrors are imminent.

'Keith,' he says, to make him turn.

'Yes?'

'Nothing.'

Balance restored, they enter together. As they walk between the beds Richard inspects the patients' faces without fear. He has that same sense of invincibility you get after your third drink. You feel capable, funny, interesting. You know you are liked.

Edith looks much better. She is propped up in bed with folded arms and a sour expression. Her face flickers when she sees Keith, but this smile doesn't linger. She quickly returns to her scowl.

Keith is still a few feet from her bed when she launches into her lament. She's being kept prisoner because although she feels fine they won't let her leave. She was dying of thirst but no one would give her a drink. She doesn't address these complaints to Richard, or seem to recognise him. He is not there for her which makes it easy for him to observe the diplomatic way Keith responds to this list of woes. He listens intently. He says he's sorry she's upset. He asks how he can help.

His patient approach would annoy you – you hate being patronised – but it works with Edith. The smoothing of her features echoes Richard's calm.

10

Of course there is no Richard, no Keith. The former is a diagnosis, the latter a cure.

11

Richard's twenty minutes late for work when he leaves Keith and Edith. He goes downstairs to Emergency and no one is angry at him because they are too busy trying to help twelve children with second- and third-degree burns. Immediately Richard is cleaning wounds and bandaging. When not doing this he speaks to their parents in a reassuring tone that makes his voice feel like air escaping a puncture. But he doesn't think of the crow or squirrel; the children's tear-stained faces do not lead to stairs. He stays upright, in the present, doing his job well. When Richard leaves at 5 a.m. he is only tired.

12

A reprieve is not salvation. When Richard enters the staffroom the following evening Grace is burning bright.

'I've swapped with Graham,' she says, then beams. As if they'd dreamt of this outcome.

'Why?' he says and opens his locker. Even through its metal door the light from her is blinding.

'I just thought it would be better,' she says coyly.

And he can think of worse things than being her captive. He feels, as you often feel, that his way of being is wrong. Something has to change, and not just drinking less coffee, eating better, taking more exercise. He wants to believe that with another person his thoughts could relax. But vertigo isn't a fear of heights; it's the terror of wanting to fall.

'I'll see you out there,' he says but doesn't make it to the door. She blocks the door with her body.

'I'm ready now,' she says, because them leaving the room together is a proof of something.

And so they begin. He, with a broken ankle, she with lacerations. Perhaps the shift won't be too bad. Although they must work in the same space, they have separate patients.

The first hour is no worse than usual. A Bradford accent

reminds him of PE, the cruelty of the showers. A faded tattoo of a blue swallow is like the one on the wrist of a builder who punched him in the neck for laughing at Elvis's film career. Unpleasant memories, but they can be managed. He swallows a single, beautiful pill. He floats and stitches and washes and comforts and every now and then he catches Grace adoring him. He doesn't mind, so long as she keeps her distance. She doesn't. She keeps interrupting with a question, a comment, all of which are individually fine, quite justifiable, but together are a dazzling series of flashes that make him want another pill because on the other side of her lights are steps named Mary, Cathy, Suzy, Gwen. All of them tried to fix him.

He is cleaning an infected toe when Grace pops her head into the cubicle to ask if he wants some fruit because she's brought in too many bananas. He wants to tell her, as nicely as possible, to leave him alone for the rest of their working lives. Instead he shakes his head, drains pus, then goes up to Edith's ward.

As soon as he enters he sees the curtain around Edith's bed. Perhaps her heart; a stroke.

When he reaches her bed he pauses but hears nothing. He thinks of Keith sitting with his head in his hands, then gently pulls back the screen. Edith has become an old man with papery skin and one eye who is lying on his back.

He closes the curtain, then finds a nurse. Edith has been discharged.

13

Edith lives in an East End council flat. If Keith is her literal neighbour, then his flat is to the left or right of hers. Richard thinks it's the one on the right because the one on the left is besieged by a collection of stone animals he cannot imagine Keith buying. Just to be sure, he knocks on the door, but there's no answer. He knocks on the other door. He waits. He just needs a glimpse of Keith.

No answer. He knocks on Edith's door, which he should have done first, because Keith is probably inside. He waits and yawns because he didn't sleep. After going back to the Emergency room he took a second pill, because it was that or push Grace into a wall. Luckily he didn't have anything skilled to do for the rest of his shift. Though he can barely remember. When he's this calm – he took a third pill on the way – there's no past or future, just an elastic now that offers immortality. (I don't know your specific fears; I'm sure you're scared of dying.)

He waits a long time. The cold is like mint. Safe and clean as snow.

When he knocks again it's without any particular hope that the result will be different. Immediately there's a sound from inside that makes him think of a shoe being banged on a wall. Through the door's frosted glass window he sees an outline approach. The door opens six inches, seeks to open wider, is yanked back by its chain. Edith's eye inspects.

'Oh, it's you.'

She removes the chain. He hears her shuffle off. He pushes the door gently and enters. He can smell baked beans.

Edith is watching television from a huge green reclining armchair next to a table heaped with celebrity magazines. Half the TV screen is covered by a yellow sweater draped over the set. As he enters the room something flickers near the curtains.

'Silly Rupert,' she says.

He doesn't know what to say. All the lines he's prepared are for scenes with Keith. He has only professional words.

'How are you feeling Edith?'

'Tired. They put me on some new statins and now I can't sleep. Why don't you sit down?'

He heads for the other armchair.

'Not there. The springs have gone. That's just for Rupert.'

He can see nowhere else to sit. Edith shakes her head. 'Move those,' she says and indicates a mound of towels that are damp to the touch. Beneath them he finds a folding wooden chair.

She laughs. 'You'd better sit lightly. It's not very strong.'

He puts the towels on Rupert's armchair, then tentatively sits. The chair protests, but holds. He asks if she's seen Keith.

'He's not here. He'll be back later. That's if he doesn't get killed on that bike of his. I've told him, it's not safe. There are maniacs, and not just on the roads.'

Rupert stirs behind the curtains but remains concealed.

Edith stares at Richard like a cake that has failed in the oven. He stands and gropes for words.

'I should be going. I'm glad you're feeling better.'

'Aren't you going to wait for Keith? I know that's why you're here.'

Richard sits. Edith's mouth cracks; wrinkles eat her eyes.

'Good,' she says. 'We can talk. Tell me about yourself.'

She might as well have handed him a knife and told him to stab himself. Whatever he says will open a door behind which steps descend. If his past contained one single, obvious trauma – a teacher with wandering hands, a father who withheld love – it might be avoided. True, his mother died of a heart attack while doing her lengths. But she was eighty-one, and apart from the drowning, did not suffer much. Though horrible, this is somehow ordinary. Many deaths are worse.

So neither he nor you can explain why sometimes breath is absent. How the heart becomes a fist trying to press its way out your chest. Yes, there are triggers, doors that lead to certain steps, but there are also days when his gaze, when your gaze is stuck to the floor. Your mouth cannot make words and yet nothing is obviously wrong. People love you. Your job is ok, you like your flat, you go on holidays, you've had sex within the last six months. You should be happy and yet, like Richard, sometimes all you want to do is lie face down on the floor, seeing, hearing nothing.

Maybe if Richard did this, pressed his face into her carpet, he could give Edith answers. He wants to. She is Keith's friend; her opinion matters. And so he risks some facts.

'I've been working at the hospital for three years. Before that I worked in a hospital in Manchester.'

She nods, apparently satisfied.

'I also live in Hackney, near the Marshes.'

Marshes as in bogs and mud. Marshes as in drowning.

'It's a good place. I don't hear the other tenants.'

She drops her head to the left. 'And what would be so bad about that? Don't they have a right to make noise?'

'Yes, of course. I just don't want to hear them.'

'Why not?'

'It disturbs me.'

'But they're just people. They're only doing normal things.'

'Yes,' he says, and nods vigorously, because Edith has to understand how much he agrees. Once she does, she will stop.

'I don't understand. Are you trying to pretend other people don't exist? That doesn't seem possible unless you go and live in the desert.'

She laughs. 'So if you find people difficult how do you cope at work? You must see a lot of us there.'

'True. But it's different. There isn't time to think.'

Which is maybe true, certainly plausible. You also need to be busy. So long as you can move from task to task, confidently grasping each like a baton, you are less likely to worry. So long as you are speaking or typing or chopping vegetables you feel in control. You don't replay a conversation, second-guess a look.

Edith moves her tongue in her mouth, then says, 'At least

you don't feel like that about everyone. I can see you've taken a shine to Keith. I can't blame you. You're not the first.'

'What do you mean?'

'People find him intriguing. Men especially.'

'I think you've got the wrong idea.'

'Have I? You couldn't take your eyes off him in the hospital. I could have been bleeding to death for all you cared.'

And sometimes you've had enough. You're sick of people talking shit about you. They have no fucking idea what it's like to try and do your job and buy groceries and get on the bus while knowing you're about to shatter.

'But you weren't bleeding to death, were you?'

'No, but it's just as well.'

'There was nothing wrong with you. You were wasting our time. While you were making a fuss to get attention there were people in real pain who needed help.'

'That's not true. That's unfair.'

'Is it? Maybe you just wanted some attention from Keith.'

Edith shakes her head. He waits for her reply. After countless frustrations, so many bruising falls, it feels incredible to push back. Just as you, when you've had enough, ignore people's calls. You do not 'like' their Facebook posts. You let their birthdays pass.

'I don't blame you. I'm guessing you don't have children. Or anyone who cares. It's just you and Rupert.'

Even though she's sitting down, he can make Edith fall.

'At your age something can happen any time. Without

Keith you could be lying here days or weeks until someone notices the smell.'

Edith looks down. She sways.

'What's wrong with you?' she says, which is a good question. Richard could say his mind connects the wrong dots; you that anxiety thrives in your chest and gut.

But Edith doesn't deserve an answer. Nor does anyone else. They smile and laugh and text you but they do not care. You are on your own.

'I'm going now,' he says and slowly stands. He savours this triumph.

'You'll never see Keith again,' she spits. 'Not after I tell him.'

'Fuck off,' he says. 'Just fuck off.' Hoping that she, as his Ambassador, will convey this message to everyone else.

Then he's out the flat and in a buffeting wind that can fuck off as well. He walks quickly, with confidence, his feet loud on the concrete stairs. He leaves the council estate, walks through a park, enters a zone of warehouses and builder's yards. The air smells of bricks, sawdust, burning rubber; trees do not exist. He's lost but knows where he's going. South, perhaps southwest, or southeast, but south nonetheless.

He is in no hurry. He's a moving point of calm. This is how he and you should feel all the time. Focussed, beyond interruption, flowing from moment to moment, sometimes ascending, sometimes going down, but smoothly. Slopes but never steps.

Not that the journey is easy. Over the next three hours

there are challenges. A difficult chin, a troubling pair of glasses; a thick moustache recalls a neighbour who used to sunbathe naked. All these doors are shut with additional pills that hone the attention until you are the only solid shape in a world of outlines. These are enough to make vectors. The rest is chaos, confusion. You do not need to see people.

Down an alley, under a bridge, through a hedge that resists. Push onto the bank of the Thames. The landscape is de-peopled. Where once were vessels, cranes and dockhands, horses, funnels, rigging, now there are cubes of glass and steel that repeat an overcast sky. Water, glass, and clouds form a single sheet. Consider its emptiness. It is completely white. Stare into a space that cannot be marked or confused. Finally, this is total focus. Lower your eyes from here.

Ward

She'd never had so many presents. Flowers, magazines, teddy bears and balloons, a poster of two puppies wedged in a boot. Sandra was the only visitor who didn't bring a gift. Her presence was confusing, because although she and Emily were in the same class at school, they definitely weren't friends. After ten minutes Emily noticed the way Sandra's eyes returned to the needle in her arm, the IV line, the slowly emptying bag. She asked if Emily was in pain, if she was going to have an operation. She wanted to tell everyone about her dying classmate.

*

It began with a scratchy throat that made her sound like Mrs Smythe who smoked in the playground. The doctor shone a light in her mouth, put his hairy hands on her throat, said, 'There's no need to worry. I'd keep her home from school a few days, but after that she should start to feel better.'

As predicted, her throat improved. That weekend she went

on a date with a boy called John who often took the same bus home. They went to the cinema and watched *The Spy Who Loved Me*. Afterwards she let him kiss her on the lips, but kept her mouth closed. He disengaged, then tried again. His tongue was half in her mouth when she pushed him away.

'No,' she said and for a moment he looked hurt. Then he lifted his fringe from his forehead. 'You're a stupid little girl. It's only a kiss.'

The soreness returned a few days later. At lunchtime her voice was a croak. By evening she had a lump in her throat that made it hurt to swallow. After examining her throat again the doctor said, 'I'd like her to see a colleague of mine.'

*

Dr Mahmoodi pushed a tube up her nose and down the back of her throat. It hurt and there was a spike of panic but then he began speaking in a voice that was English and not.

'Emily, you're doing very well. This won't take long.'

He was from Egypt, or somewhere like it, and that made the moment less real.

'Did you know that your nose has a floor?' he said. 'Or that there is a part called 'The Fossa of Rosenmuller'? I remember learning that in medical school and thinking it was beautiful.'

She thought of him younger, with more hair, surrounded by Pyramids. Then he went quiet and she felt the end of the tube shift. He was looking at a part of her she would never see.

'All done,' he said and she felt the tube begin to retreat, slowly, steadily, and she wanted to laugh because she was thinking of the game they had at the harvest fair where you had to guide a brass ring down a crooked wire without making a buzzer sound.

'Well done,' he said. 'I think everything's fine. But I'd like to be sure.'

*

They were going to cut out a piece of her throat while she was asleep.

She walked with her mother down corridors where everything was calm. She wanted to hold her mother's hand but knew she was too old.

She put on a smock. She waited. The sun was coming through the window onto the floor at her feet. It was a Wednesday and they would be playing hockey at school.

Two nurses passed talking loudly.

'Gary's a pig,' said one.

'A handsome pig,' said her colleague, and laughed.

The other nurse shrugged. 'I don't care what Becky did. She didn't deserve that.'

'True,' said the other, then Emily's mother stood up. The trolley had arrived.

She got on the trolley and after a moment the ceiling was flowing so smoothly it was like the floor. She was running, avoiding the lights, jumping over doorframes. She was gliding on a ride she didn't want to stop.

They stopped. Doors opened. The lights became too bright.

'We're going to move you,' said a man and then hands went round her shoulders and ankles.

Her mother obscured the light. She took Emily's hand.

'Darling, you're going to feel a little prick and then you'll be asleep. I'll be here with you.'

But the needle really hurt. 'Why don't you start counting?' said a woman.

Emily said the first numbers, then began to struggle. Her tongue was a lump that muddled the sounds but so long as she was thinking *twelve* it didn't matter what came out. If she was saying *welf, theteen*, it meant she was awake and there was no knife in her throat. She squeezed her mother's hand and counted; when she got to *wenty oo* she felt she'd won. She'd keep going, past a hundred, till the doctors left.

Afterwards, when she was under, the anaesthetist told her mother that people were usually asleep before they got to ten.

'Has anyone else got that far?'

He smiled at her question. 'Oh yes.'

*

She had cancer of the larynx. They kept doing tests. They put her through a ring that turned and made a noise like a vacuum cleaner. They took blood and urine and put the tube up her nose and still the result did not change. She had cancer of the larynx.

*

She lay on her back and received radiation. Sometimes she thought she could feel the green fog of it moving through her throat, disturbing its tissues. As for what it was doing to the tumour, she had no idea. The lump didn't feel smaller; her voice was just as hoarse. The irritation of the skin on her neck was the only noticeable change.

After four weeks her radiotherapist decided she should have two sessions a day. 'It will give you the best chance,' he said.

Two weeks later, she was admitted to hospital.

*

Queen Mary's children's ward had posters and toys and coloured lines on the floor. The red line led to the room where she was weighed, the yellow to the room where they took blood. She didn't know where the blue one went.

She didn't belong on the ward. Most of the other patients were younger; when she looked at them she felt as if she was twenty or thirty. Even the ones with broken legs and bandaged heads seemed certain to recover. There were only two patients that seemed as ill as her. Matthew had yellowish skin and sunken eyes and looked like the teenagers on TV who hadn't said no to drugs. His kidneys were failing. Most of the time the screens were drawn around his bed; when they were open she saw him lying on his side while scratching his arms. At night she could hear the muffled squeak of his crying.

The other unfortunate was Rashida. When Emily first saw her she seemed like a normal seven-year-old girl sitting on a hospital bed. She was wondering why the girl was wearing a hat on a warm day till she took it off. Then she saw Rashida's shaved head, and the cannula stuck in her scalp. Rashida said it didn't hurt, and called it 'my chimney', but it was monstrous, a horrible experiment performed by a mad scientist.

But eventually Emily got used to it. On her way back from the red or yellow line she would stop and sit with Rashida, usually for a game of draughts or snap, but sometimes just to keep her company while she played in a world of her own. Although she had been in the ward for longer than Emily, and was regularly visited, she didn't seem to have many toys.

One afternoon when Emily was lying on her bed, her hand on her throat, she inspected all her presents lined up on the cupboard. There was a bear, a panda, a yellow goose, two cats with very long whiskers. There was a pink elephant with fluffy fur, a seal holding a tennis racquet. Her relatives had meant well. But having cancer didn't mean she was a little girl again.

She swung her legs to the floor then gathered most of the toys. She took them to Rashida and said, 'Is it your birthday?'

'Yes,' she said, although it almost certainly wasn't, then put the cat on the elephant. Emily didn't think Rashida's parents would mind. As for hers, if they noticed the toys were gone, they probably wouldn't say.

*

Emily watched Dr Stewart's mouth explain the risks of a partial laryngectomy. She would have problems swallowing and eating. Her voice would be affected. When her mother asked if this would be permanent, the doctor's lips compressed.

'Unfortunately we can't say for sure.'

As if it were a secret.

Her father pushed a hand through his hair; when he spoke he sounded annoyed.

'But will it definitely work?'

The doctor wetted her lips. 'In most cases the earlier we operate, the better the chance of a full recovery.'

'So if it isn't going to work, why should she—' Her mother interrupted. 'Just tell us which has a better chance, surgery or more radiotherapy.'

The doctor took a moment before answering, 'Mr and Mrs Tryb, I know this is a very difficult decision. I can't tell you that either of these options are guaranteed to work. She's had a lot of radiotherapy, and it hasn't shrunk the tumour, and I don't think it's going to. If Emily were my daughter, I would want her to have the surgery. But I can only advise you.'

While her parents talked, and while her mother cried, Emily thought *I want to be a doctor.*

*

She spent most the next day in quiet places where she spoke to herself out loud. They weren't proper conversations, just simple phrases like 'How are you?' and 'That's wonderful.' She wanted to remember her voice.

*

She followed the yellow line, then the red. Several hours later she got on a trolley and followed the blue line down the corridor, round the bend, through two sets of doors, till they passed beneath a sign that read 'Theatre'. She thought of Romeo and Juliet, how they'd been no older than her.

*

Tracheotomy *n.* (*pl.* tracheotomies) *Medicine-* an incision in the windpipe made to relieve an obstruction to breathing.

*

She woke in the dark that wasn't dark because there was always a light at night on the ward. A tube was cutting into her throat. There was a needle in her arm and a bad taste in her mouth and the walls had changed. The tube was hurting, cutting deeper; the ceiling was higher, the walls closer. The

windows were different shapes and open because there was
the sound of the wind whistling. Yet there was no draught,
it was not cold, and still the noise rose and fell. It was the
breathing tube they had put into her throat after cutting out
part of her larynx which contained cells that wouldn't die
and didn't care if their living killed her. The cells had smiley
faces and were pleased to be living and she wanted the pain
to stop. Although this bed wasn't her bed on the ward – how
many had died in it? – it must have buttons that could call a
nurse. Some of them glowed – a lightbulb, a box – but these
were useless because she didn't want to watch TV or read.
She wanted the stick figure that led to a person who'd make
the pain stop.

She tried one of the buttons without a label; when nothing
happened she jabbed at another, a third, and as she breathed
the wind whistled. She was dying in this room on her own
in the middle of the night. She thought of her parents stood
round her grave, her father pale, her mother sobbing, while
that vulture Sandra kept whispering, 'I knew she didn't have
long left.'

'She's coming,' said a man. His voice was old and she didn't
know why he was at her funeral.

'It's alright. She'll give you something.'

There was a shift in the dark, a friction of fabric, the
scuffing scrape of slippers. A cold hand caressed her brow.
There was a hole in the dark. 'This will help you sleep,' said
the nurse and this at least was true.

*

For the next two days she was only a throat. The swelling around the wound was like a choking hand.

Her parents visited, bringing more children's toys. They smiled and spoke of normal things – new plants; the car was acting up – while their eyes flicked to, then from, the tube stuck in her throat.

Her mother said, 'I don't know why they had to move you. This ward is so old. We really should complain.'

'It's a hospital, not a hotel,' said her father. 'And this ward is for recovery. It's much quieter.'

'But not as clean,' snapped her mother then her face seemed to collapse.

Having passed her swallow evaluation, they gave her a feeding tube. Three times a day Nurse Maynard brought her a milkshake that came in three flavours of chalk. After half of it she wanted to stop, but Nurse Maynard was always firm.

'You have to keep up your strength,' she said, and waited for Emily to finish. When, on the third day, she refused to drink, the nurse said, 'Drink up. There are starving children in Africa who'd be glad of it.'

If she wasn't force-feeding Emily, she was draining fluid from her wound. Emily knew these were necessary tasks. But it was good to have someone to hate.

*

Emily was staring at the wall when she heard the voice of the man who had stood at her grave. It was painful to turn over – after four days, the swelling remained – but she wanted to see what he looked like.

He was old and almost bald except for grey tufts by his ears. He had a cane and thick glasses. He was talking to Nurse Maynard but not looking at her face. His gaze was aimed lower, at her breasts, and although this was disgusting, Emily didn't blame him. He was probably dying too.

He laughed, but only briefly, because this started him coughing, and then he had to sit down. It was a harsh sound that made her think of the serrated spoons her father used on his grapefruit. The old man coughed over and over, the noise scraping its way out, till he was gasping for breath. Nurse Maynard quickly got an oxygen mask on his face and turned the cylinder on. He clutched it to his face and took deep breaths; she'd never seen the simple act of breathing look so enjoyable.

*

The following day the old man stopped and spoke as if they knew each other.

'How is it? Can you talk?'

Emily shook her head. This was a lie, because she could whisper. But her voice sounded wrong.

'Can I sit with you a moment? Would that be annoying?'

He was Irish, but with such a faint accent she hadn't heard it at first.

'My name's Gordon. And I basically live here. I'm practically married to Nurse Maynard though she doesn't know it yet. Is your name Emily?'

She nodded.

'I thought I heard your mother say it. It's a wonderful name. I knew an Emily when I was a boy in Sligo. She ended up marrying a friend of mine who was a farmer and together they had a litter of pigs.'

It was stupid, but she smiled.

'And maybe one or two cows. No, wait.' He raised a finger. 'I think those were adopted.'

He paused as if in contemplation of their menagerie. Then he leaned forward.

'So you have cancer?'

She hesitated before nodding. As if this was still private.

'Very nasty, so sorry,' he said. She was disappointed when his face slackened and he looked away. It was how most reacted. Like her answer had to be the end of the conversation.

'Terrible,' he said. 'But you'll get your voice back. And there'll be other summers, not that you can really call them 'summer'. More like the monsoon.'

Even her parents didn't dare speak this way. They were positive, upbeat and cheerful; but they were careful with hope. As for the doctors, everything was qualified. They made no promises. She knew that if she got better, it could still come back.

'What's the matter?' he asked.

She tried to cry from only her eyes, with her mouth clamped shut, but the tears burned her throat. The idea she might have a future – might sing in the bath, kiss a boy with her tongue – was just as upsetting as the thought of dying, probably even more so. These were real things that she could imagine.

'Here,' said Gordon. He handed her a pink tissue. 'I'm sorry, that was probably my stupid mouth. It has no link with my brain.'

He turned his head to cough; the first was a normal, shallow sound; the next was a wheeze. Emily was about to press the call button when he shook his head. He bent over, pressed his palm into his chest, coughed three times then stopped. He swallowed and looked pale.

She pointed at her throat, then him.

'No.' He swallowed again, took a cautious breath. 'Emphysema. And a problem with my waterworks.'

She raised her eyebrows.

'Trust me, you don't want to know. Be glad it won't happen to you.'

She didn't know what he meant, and was about to whisper, but then Nurse Maynard interrupted.

*

After a week, the swelling went down. She was allowed soft food.

*

On a rainy afternoon they sat by the window and she listened
to him talk. He had been in the merchant navy, then the fire
brigade. He had a great love of dogs.

'Never met a bad one. Some were scared, some unhappy,
but that was down to people.'

It had been raining since morning. The bushes and trees
were so vibrantly green they seemed cocky.

Gordon said he had been married twice but talked about
three women. Each of their names was said with a reverence
laced with disbelief. First was Caitlin, then Iona, and at some
point, maybe overlapping, there was Maureen. It was easy to
imagine him younger, her father's age, his hair returned, dark
and thick, all his wrinkles smooth. She saw him walking arm
in arm with one of them through the woods. If the path was
quiet, and no one was coming, they would lean together and
kiss with their mouths open. He'd put his arm round her,
draw her tight and then—

'Do you know what I mean?'

'Oh yes,' she said, although she hadn't been listening. To
change the subject she asked the first thing that popped into
her head.

'What did your first wife look like?'

'Oh,' he said, and shook his head slightly, 'She was the
most beautiful girl in our village. At least me and the other
men thought so. She was tall and had great cheekbones and

the best nose I've seen. It was like a pretty shell stuck on her face. Her hair was brown, a bit like yours, maybe darker, but about the same length. You know I think you look a bit like her. I'm not saying you're her twin, just related that's all.'

She blushed and looked out into the garden, then felt stupid for doing so. John had been right. She should have let him kiss her properly. There was no reason not to. He was good looking and older and her classmates would have been impressed. She could have gone to the park with him and kissed for hours, what her classmate Maxine called 'sucking face'. She wasn't sure how far she'd let him go; but kissing and touching were fine. She'd been stupid to be scared, she could taste—

'Am I right? On Saturday?'

'What?'

'You'd think you'd remember. That's when they're sending you home.'

'I think so,' she said. It seemed bad manners to speak of leaving to someone who had to stay.

She turned her face and held his eyes, what would normally have been a stare. But at that moment it felt permitted; this was her last look.

'Well, good luck out there,' he said. 'Send me a postcard.'

*

There was a light but it was still dark, not morning. 'Relax,' said a woman and Emily worried. Hands were at her throat.

They applied white pads of dressing that came away red. There were too many hands for one person, there must be a man, a handsome pig, putting his trotters on her.

'More pressure,' he said and Emily gasped because she had been stabbed. A perfectly sharp pencil straight from the box had been shoved into her throat. It had gone through, pinned her to the pillow, punctured her as if she were an inflatable doll. The air was leaving her, rushing out, there was none left to breathe, she couldn't

*

'Don't worry,' said Dr Stewart. 'It can happen. You must have caught the tube. We'll keep you in a few days more.'

*

Her temperature rose in hurried leaps that defied the drugs. She was feverish and her lips were dry and she was cold and she was hot. They said it was an infection but they were lying. It was cancer and only a stupid little girl could have believed otherwise.

It became too painful to eat. When she looked at the IV line she felt like a plant. Something to be watered, fed, kept out of the fucking light.

*

Sleeping was the only thing she liked. Long ago, when she'd been well, it had seemed a waste of time. Now there was nothing better. The screen round her bed made her claustrophobic, but the view of the ward, its beds and nurses, the circus of sickness, was as irritating as a bad film she had already seen. Even the sight of her parents was enough to anger her. They had nothing new to say, there was nothing they could do, and yet they kept coming with stupid books and toys and talk about people and things that would never matter again. When her mother mentioned that Maxine had been in a car accident, and was now on crutches, Emily snapped at her.

'So what? At least she'll get better.'

Her mother burst into tears, then apologised, which was all wrong because it was Emily's fault. But instead of putting a hand on her mother's arm, croaking out a few soft words, she remained mute and watched her mother's shoulders jerk.

*

First she felt a pulse so short she barely noted it. A heart's fast blip; a shooting star; a raindrop racing down glass.

But a single note, played separately, does not divert a song. She had been listening to its melody for several days, or maybe just one, it no longer mattered. The melody was so constant it took shape from her routine. Whether it was light or dark, quiet or noisy, she was within pain.

The second pulse was twice as long; the third was lights

flicking on in the rooms of an abandoned house. What had been dark, lifeless, given up on, became sources of warmth. As the heat spread through her body there was a rush of sensation.

The sheets lay gentle on her skin.

Her fingers seemed to glow.

Between her thighs, where they touched, she felt a low vibration.

Her head was swollen, full of air; floating fast away.

This was her first taste of morphine.

*

They did another biopsy. They were playing let's-pretend. She was getting worse every day and yet nothing was said. The closest they came was when Dr Stewart said, 'We're going to make you more comfortable.' This meant she got more morphine. Three days passed in a blur in which only two incidents stood out. One was hearing Gordon say her name while underwater. She didn't know why or how he was there, but it was very funny, it was hilarious, yet she couldn't laugh.

The second incident was more fuzzy. She was flying over mountains and yet could hear a phone ringing as she looked down without fear. The mountains weren't really mountains; they were giant pillars of living stone somewhere in China. They were thousands of years old, as was she, she'd had so many children they were all the living people in the world (or at least China). She was very hot because she was near to the sun, and flying, how she didn't know and suddenly it mattered more than anything else. Panicked, she searched her body, expecting wings or some other device; although there was nothing unusual, the touch of herself was reassuring. Her belly, her thighs, the hug of them of her hand. Her body was solid, familiar; if nothing else, she was real. She was real and flying who knows how above an epic landscape that demanded music. And so she sang to herself, but didn't bother with words, just a low, long note that welled up from her centre. It was so deep and loud a moan that there were echoes, both from below, and from inside, and they felt amazing. She was weightless, incandescent, never more alive.

When she woke the screens were round the bed. When Nurse Maynard came to check on her, she didn't make eye contact. It was as if she was embarrassed.

*

Gordon died from complications. They said she was clear. She did not know which was less believable.

But there was evidence for both. He did not come and sit by her bed. Her wound began to heal.

'You'll have a scar,' said Dr Stewart and she found this pleasing. She wanted people to wonder.

She spent another week in hospital, then they sent her home.

Emily spent the next two weeks at home, and was very bored for the first. She couldn't get past the opening chapter of every book she tried. A girl loved a boy or a boy loved a girl or there was some kind of ridiculous adventure that could never happen. They were boring, nothing happened, or at least nothing important. In desperation she went and found a book in her mother's room. It was called *Flowers in the Attic* and told the story of a brother and sister kept captive in an attic. They almost starved to death and had to eat mice and then had sex with each other. She couldn't put it down.

'I'm not sure you should be reading that,' said her mother.

'Why not?'

'It's really for adults.'

So's cancer, thought Emily.

*

There were only two weeks left of school but she still went back. Much was said about the importance of Emily getting back to normal.

For the first few days she was the centre of attention. Her classmates wanted to know how she was feeling, if she was better, if she had been scared. She gave up trying to tell them what it had been like. They were healthy, pleasant girls who couldn't understand.

But she was pleased when Maxine sat next to her at lunch. Although Maxine asked the same questions, they sounded better coming from her beautiful face. Emily wanted to put a fingertip on the bulge of her cheekbone. Beneath the skin she'd feel a pulse of energy.

For the next ten days they sat together. Maxine had to do most of the talking, but didn't seem to mind. Emily often slipped beneath her purling stream of words. She looked at the elvish features and wondered how many boys Maxine had actually kissed. Definitely one – it had been witnessed – but that was probably all. It was hard to imagine she'd gone further. Emily couldn't imagine her in a park, or the back of a car, being touched by a *boy*. When it happened he would be older, a teacher, a friend of her father, someone who knew they shouldn't but couldn't help himself.

But although Maxine wasn't like the other girls, she wasn't like Emily either. On the last day of term, when Maxine said, too keenly, 'I hope we can see each other in the holidays,' Emily answered quickly.

'I'd really like that,' she said. 'But we're going away all summer.'

*

This lie turned out to be true. A few days later her father and mother said they had a surprise. A week later they were driving, then on a ferry, then driving again. They saw a candy-striped chimney belching smoke. As they passed through northern France her father played the same tape over and over but she didn't mind. Though the trees and the roads and the cars and the houses were not so different from those at home, what kept her face pressed to the window was that they were new.

They spent the night in a little town called Saint Omer. For dinner she ate a steak that looked burnt but was mostly full of blood. It was the best meat she had ever tasted.

In the night it rained so heavily that she woke and did not know where she was. For a groggy moment, as she blinked in the dark, she thought of the ward. She recalled the firm handshake of Dr Stewart. She remembered Gordon. They were clear in her mind, and yet also distant, as if it had all happened so long ago. She concentrated, trying to conjure their faces, but water was striking something metal on the balcony, making it ring loud as a bell. No sooner did she form their faces, then the sound destroyed them.

In the morning the sky was clear and this was how it stayed. They drove on long featureless roads they had to pay to use. There was little to see, because there were high banks either side, and her mother soon nodded off. Her father occasionally checked on Emily in the mirror but said little. He seemed content to be driving fast on a straight road while listening to Chopin.

She didn't mind his silence. After weeks lying in bed, she was happy to be moving. She didn't want to arrive.

Which made the thirty-five minutes they spent in the service station excruciating. Her mother dawdled, picking up a doll in a tube, a tea towel, a series of magazines although she couldn't read French. It was a waste of time better spent hurtling at speeds impossible in England. It was stupid, just like the shop and all the ugly, boring things it sold, and there was only one response. Emily picked up a pack of playing cards and took out several just enough to tear them. Having done so, she shoved them back in and moved on to the dolls. The hair came off their heads so easily.

*

Their holiday cottage was in a long valley made by broad shouldered hills. During the day they were so green they seemed capable of growth. After the sun set they became purple holes in the world. There were birds with strange calls and flitting bats and her mother and father kept sighing as they drank red wine on the terrace. 'Can we stay here forever?' they took it in turns to ask, and she was happy for them. They needed a holiday as much as she did. They needed to be in this beautiful, relaxing place and it wasn't their fault that it made her feel like a pillow was being held over her face. If she'd known how to drive she would already be in Nice, Marseilles, or even Italy. The road would wind forever and on and she would move with it, through the towns, between the fields, over misty mountains, rivers, seas, till the lines of the kingdoms were blurred. Living things needed to move.

Laurent was the son of the couple who owned the cottage. He had shoulder-length black curly hair, a fleshy mouth, and was usually smoking in a hammock strung between two oaks. He was twenty-two or three, and handsome, though not in an obvious way. His features were asymmetrical, or his eyes too far apart, or maybe they were just too French. His main activities were smoking and looking incredibly bored by Emily and her parents. When they returned from their trip to a vineyard, or chateaux, he raised his head just enough to be disappointed by the sight of them. 'You'd think he'd get bored of brooding,' her mother said.

He had only spoken to Emily once. She had been sunbathing on the terrace when she felt herself in shade. At first she thought of a cloud blocking the sun, then a whiff of cigarette smoke found its way to her. She heard a noise that wasn't a word, which she attempted to imitate later. She tried a tutting sound, but that wasn't it; the closest she got was having her tongue between her teeth then drawing it sharply back. As for what it meant, she had no idea. It could have been a suck of disapproval, or merely accidental.

*

She trudged round the Chateau de Gascon, sulked through the Chateau de Ville; when she said she wasn't coming to Chateau Esteffe her parents said 'Alright'. They drove off after breakfast, happy, seeming so much younger that she could finally accept the oft-told story of them driving round Europe on their honeymoon. Until then it had been a fact acknowledged without being wholly believed.

She read *The Prime of Miss Jean Brodie* for an hour then had to put it down and sit by the river. The book was good but too upsetting: when it told of how a girl would one day die in a fire on a train, it almost seemed to be laughing at her.

The water was rich and brown and she thought of the flames. Spreading fast through the compartments, seeming to race the train. If the girl (by then a woman) had time to try and escape, she might have been looking at the blur of the tracks, preparing to jump, when the fire took her. How long did it take to burn to death? Would Emily recognise that pain? She thought of blackened skin and choking, the feeling of being engulfed by an uncaring heat.

The woman screamed as she burned and she had Maxine's face, which was wrong; Emily made her less pretty. Sandra, older, screamed and burned but the image was still upsetting.

Emily stood and stepped out of her shoes; she threw herself off the river bank. After the impact, there was silence, water pushing at her ears; an erasure of previous thought. By the time she surfaced she was calm again. Everything made sense. She wasn't burning, and probably wouldn't; maybe she'd be healthy for fifteen or twenty years.

The water was cold, so she started swimming, but something felt wrong. She took her t-shirt off and threw it on the bank. She resumed swimming, and it felt much better – more smooth – and then she saw Laurent. He was thirty feet upstream, ostensibly reading a book, but must have known she was there. How long had he been watching? Had he seen her remove her shirt?

Even if he had, it had only been for a second, and since then she had been submerged. She wasn't going to worry what some lazy French boy might (or might not) have glimpsed. Besides, she was surely too young for him even though this was France where people married their 15-year-old cousins.

She swam in slow, tight circles till her legs were warm then realised she was hungry. She'd have the half baguette left over from breakfast with paté and cheese. It would be an amazing lunch; her only problem was getting out the water without being seen.

She waited ten minutes, hoping Laurent would leave, but he showed no signs of doing so. Though he kept reading, he now occasionally glanced in her direction, as if knowing what to expect. Emily swam back and forth, her irritation mounting while her hunger grew. There was definitely no way for her to get out the river without him seeing her virtually naked.

Once she accepted this there was only one thing to do. She stood without particular haste and moved toward the bank. When she got out she picked up her top but didn't bother putting it on. What was the point? It would only suggest that she cared whether or not he saw her breasts. Nonetheless, her heart was beating fast as she bent and picked up her book, but again she took care to do so slowly. She wasn't going to act like a scared little English girl.

She started up the slope of the garden; only at the last moment before he disappeared from view did she glance in his direction. Laurent was still reading.

After the sunlight the kitchen was so dim she had to wait for her eyes to adjust. She stood, her heart still beating fast, hearing bird song from outside, suddenly finding it hard to believe that she, who had been dying of cancer, could now feel so vital. It was something healthy people wouldn't understand.

She took the food from the fridge, then stood in front of it, feeling it cool her skin. There was an open bottle of white wine and it looked so icy, so refreshing, that she didn't hesitate. It tasted crisp and dry and she wanted all of it, and what could they do? But at the very least, they would talk and talk, asking why she had done that. If it didn't spoil her holiday, it would ruin theirs. So she closed the fridge and slit the bread and filled it with cheese and pate. She was about to go outside to eat when she saw the bottle of red wine on the counter. It wasn't cold, but tasted like ripe fruit, so she drank as much from it as she had the white.

The light outside was a bully, pushing down her eyes. She spread a blanket on the grass then lay down to eat. By the time she'd finished the sunlight was heavy on her head, firmly pushing it down. She lay on her back, eyes closed, fingering the scar at her throat. The sun was hot but she didn't mind; she could absorb it all. She thought of how her body must look to the birds, its patchwork of light and brown, the invitation of the berry placed on either side. She pinched her nipples, once, twice, thought of closing beaks, then laughed. Those birds would be surprised.

The footsteps did not alarm her. She could lay there, her chest exposed; if it bothered him that wasn't her problem.

He said her name, and she didn't know how he knew it, but it sounded good with his accent. When she opened her eyes he was kneeling next to her. He put his hand on her chest, and she didn't mind, nor when his mouth touched hers. It was just kissing and touching, things she was going to do one day so why not now? His tongue moved slowly, gently, while his hand explored. When his hand arrived between her legs he took his mouth away. He looked into her eyes and said, 'OK?'

*

They had almost a week together before they were discovered. It was a very long drive back to Calais but her father didn't play any tapes. They drove in silence except for when her mother or father hurled words at her.

The rest of that summer was hot and boring because she had no money and wasn't supposed to go anywhere, although she did, because they couldn't lock her up. After two weeks of sitting in libraries, wandering around shops, she met a man in the park. His name was Clive and he was about forty, and he was much better than Laurent. He had the keys to a lock up close to the park in which there was a car with no wheels, and after the first few times, a mattress without sheets. They met every day for three weeks, always at lunchtimes – she thought he must work close by – until one day he didn't show up. She went back to the park for the next three days but never saw him again.

But she had learnt her lesson. There were men she only had to stare at for long enough and they would approach her. The oldest was sixty-five, maybe older, and smelt like cough syrup. When they were doing it he seemed to be in shock.

After two weeks back at school she was suspended; after a month she was expelled. At home she rarely made it through a meal without storming out. She had exchanged death for a prison sentence. Nothing at school, home, or any place else seemed capable of letting her properly live.

She was arrested for stealing a shirt that wouldn't even have fit her.

On her sixteenth birthday she got in a lorry going north.

She worked in cafes, hotels, and restaurants. She got pregnant, but not for long. Over the next twenty years she slept with kind men, men that spoke little English, men who let her treat them like shit. There were men that hit her, men that cut her, men who choked her in a way that she did not enjoy. She had joyous, loving sex every day for weeks while camping in a Bavarian forest. She said, 'Will you marry me?' while riding in a boxcar. She lived with three other women in a flat in Amsterdam with high, curved ceilings that made her think of an upturned boat. In bed there was nothing she was afraid of, nothing she had not done. Only when she was an old woman, living by herself in a house by the Black Sea, did it occur to her, as the breeze lifted the scent from the flowers, that with all these men and women, no matter what they did with their dicks, tongues and fingers, however profound her orgasm, there was something lacking. The pleasure was always incomplete; never quite like morphine.

The False River

Number of this bus: the 6838, which starts in L.A. and runs to Sacramento.

Number of passengers: 33, which is less than two-thirds full.

Number of black people: 20.

Number of white people: 8.

Number of people whose ethnicity cannot be determined without closer inspection: 5.

Number of men: 22.

Number of women: 11, 3 of whom are elderly. Judging from their expressions – please-don't-rob-or-kill-me – they have never taken the bus before.

Number of the remaining 8 who are more than averagely pretty: 4. All but one of these 4 are with a man who is unlikely to be a platonic friend, cousin or brother, judging by the acts they've performed: a slow kiss; a slap on the ass; making her sit on his lap. For safety reasons, the latter was asked to desist, at first in a firm though friendly manner, then (on the second occasion) in a much stricter tone, and finally, 5 minutes ago, with a yell and a threat.

Number of more than averagely pretty women with hair so long and blonde and bright it looks as if she's in some old religious painting where the women are angels or saints: 1.

Number of people talking on cell phones: 9.

Number of people with headphones in their ears: 10. The rest stare out at the sky which is full of clouds. I do not think there is much rain in them. A shower that will cleanse, but not drench. Dust will be washed from the chrome and the windows. The sun will reflect in so brilliant a fashion that even the most jaded observer will look on the shining road and feel that though there are no guarantees (and rarely grounds for optimism), there are, and always must be, chances for things to happen which transform a life.

Number of miles till we reach Modesto: 30.

Number of places in Modesto services where two people might enjoy a cup of coffee: 2. The chicken place has the best coffee, so long as Hector is working. Otherwise, it's the burger joint whose coffee is tepid or scalding. But the coffee doesn't have to be great, so long as it's not terrible. Then it could be an unpleasant distraction from their conversation. If, for instance, the man is saying something important to the woman – a sentiment that began as a rough rock, which now, after weeks of being handled, is a smooth feeling he wishes to pass on – he will not want it distorted by a cup of coffee that tastes so awful it coats his words with oily, bitter drops. Then there might be a misunderstanding. She could get the wrong idea. She might think I—

Number of times the red sedan in front has signalled, started to pull out, then cowardly hung back: 3.

Minimum number of times the woman with hair you really have to call *golden* (a woman whose name, according to the manifest, is Dominique Stitz) has taken the bus this month: 9. She could have also taken it on either the 3 days I was off sick, or the 2 I was in court.

Number of times we have spoken: 9. When I take her ticket, she says, 'Thank you,' then gets on the bus. I have never seen her smile, laugh, show any sign her life is not a miserable, long tunnel.

And sadness looks worse on a face like hers. It's a contradiction. This is a face you *want* to be happy, one that could make even the most callous person — someone who robs the poor box; mocks the disabled; sleeps with the wife of his best friend while he drives a 55 hour week — stop her in the street and ask, *Whatever is the matter?*

Number of miles to Modesto: 20.

Number of words I will say to Dominique as she climbs off the bus: 19. 'I hope you don't mind me asking but— Would you like to have a cup of coffee with me?'

Number of words she will reply: 4. As in, 'Yes, I'd like that.' Or 3, as in, 'Sure, why not?' And contrary to popular belief, there isn't a number, like 7, or 13, that's *always* lucky or not. It depends on the person and the situation. There are definitely trends, for sure, but nothing's cast in stone. For example, while 9 has mostly been bad for me – I met my ex-wife on September 9th; there are 9 letters in her name, and 9 letters in *his* name – there are also 9 letters in Dominique, this is the 9th time we've met, and we're on Highway 99. So while it's good to be aware of these things, you shouldn't let them freak you out. Not unless you want to end up like my Dad (who stays home on days that contain a '1' or '3').

Number of miles to Modesto: 15. I do not expect much. There

will be no hugs or kisses. We are just going to talk. After our names, we'll say where we're from, what we do for a living (as a joke, I'll say I'm a lawyer). Then, after an awkward pause, it will all come out. The months of suspicion; my wife's affair; the divorce. What Charmaine said in court.

Then it will be Dominique's turn. A betrayal, an accident, the death of someone dear: whatever the tragedy, the words will just flood out. She will find herself saying things she never thought she could. Because she'll see that we are the same. Broken people ill-treated by life who still cannot give up.

Number of times the man in front of her has laughed: 4. He is reading a book or newspaper, I can't tell which from here. He is in his late-twenties, with a short beard and glasses. I'm guessing he's a student.

Number of signs for Big Don's Chicken between Turlock and Modesto: 5

Number of times Charmaine's attorney said 'mental cruelty' during the hearing: 24.

Number of times Dominique has looked up, no doubt in annoyance, at the excessive laughter from the man in front of her: 3. It's all very well to enjoy things, but. After a point, it's look-at-me-and-all-the-fun-*I'm*-having.

Correction. There are now 6 signs for Big Don's Chicken. The new one features his face on a 10-foot rooster brandishing a drumstick. The big nose, coupled with his red cheeks, is enough of a resemblance for my hands to spasm on the wheel, and the bus to lurch to the side. Apart from the elderly woman – who opens her eyes, looks around, shuts them – the only other person to notice is the bearded man who waves his hands in the air. He says something, then laughs, and when Dominique laughs too I am so taken aback by the sound – as warm as wine held in the mouth – that I almost forget about Big Don, or rather the man that Big Don resembles. Jefferson and I had been friends since 10th grade.

Number of times I hit him: 15. The branch was from an oak we were supposed to finish pruning. If rain hadn't flooded the road, if I hadn't come back 2 hours early, the 2 of us would probably have got that tree down to 4 branches.

Number of miles to Modesto: 5.

Number of times Dominique has laughed: 11. Which, like the number 9, is not a good number for me. It was the brand of lotion Charmaine used to rub on her feet. The lotion was pink and smelt of mint and there wasn't a name on the bottle, only these 2 thick vertical lines which looked so black against the pink that they were like the bars of a cage within which there was not a creature, or person, but instead some substance of pure evil.

We pull into Modesto. 'Be back in 15,' I say. Then Dominique's out of her seat. She is moving down the aisle, closing the distance between us. *Now*, I think, and form the words. But she has come from two-thirds back, so although she makes it past several rows, the aisle is soon blocked. An old woman with coke-bottle glasses pats her coat and looks round in a puzzled fashion. As if her youth had only been mislaid, forgotten in some pocket. While she searches she smiles and apologises for being in people's way, but despite this, does not hurry her hands.

The old woman touches her face, then sighs with pleasure. 'There they are,' she says then steps out of the aisle.

And Dominique is like a popped cork: past and swiftly down the steps as I say her name.

There is an interval I do not count. When I stand and watch them file past while I stand there, stunned. And this is the worst part of a slap: the fucking surprise of it.

I could just stay in my seat. Say it was never going to happen on meeting number 9. But despite what Charmaine said, I am not a slave to numbers. If I counted the words in her sentences, the fries on her plate, it was only because I liked the patterns they made.

I get off then lock the cab. I walk across the forecourt. As soon as the doors slide open, I smell the grease, the fat.

Hector is behind the counter, tossing bits of chicken. As I approach he turns and reaches for the coffee pot. 'Steven,' he says and pours then puts the cup by me. 'Thanks Hector,' I say. I slide him a bill, he slides it back, and then I scan the room. The window tables are full of spinsters (15), with 3, no, 4 men sitting amongst them, meek and silent pets. Apart from them, at other tables, are my passengers: the forgetful old woman, the amorous couple (she on his lap again), the bearded man with the smug face. There they are. But she is not. And there are 9, 10, 11 seconds when I imagine her in the trunk of some man's car. Darkness and the smell of oil. Her misery ending all wrong.

Then it is the scene in *Taxi Driver* where Cybil Shepherd floats in slow motion while De Niro says, *'They... Cannot... Touch... Her...'*

She is perfect. Untouchable. But nonetheless, so sad. I don't know if I can make her happy. If I have the words.

I step forward. She approaches. Then sits quickly down.

She is next to the bearded man whose eyes are wide with surprise, as mine must be as they close.

I count the panicked beats of my heart. The pulse of pain in my chest.

When, at 20, I open my eyes, she is no longer kissing him. They are kissing each other.

I watch their lips for many seconds that I do not count. Then I go back to the bus and sound the horn so loud that people spill their drinks. I start the engine and watch the passengers scurry to the bus. All except Dominique and him, who 10, 15 seconds later, almost skip between the sliding doors and here. At me they do not even glance. I am less than these spots of rain.

It cannot be me who says, 'Next stop, Stockton.' Who swings the bus out into the road with barely a look in the mirror. But even that is enough. The two of them are entwined. His hands on her, his lips on her. This man who knows nothing of sadness. Who probably believes that books can offer better worlds. The last book I managed to finish was a children's story someone left on the bus. It was called *The crocodile's birthday party*. Many animals came to the party, all of them dressed in fine clothes. There were songs, cake, and games. Then the crocodile ate his guests. Hungrily and with as much pleasure as she is sucking his mouth.

It will be 32 miles to Stockton. Half an hour through rain. And why did she? How *could* she? Maybe she thinks they'll do new things together, things that don't connect with her past. They will go bowling; they will go camping; they will run through flower-filled meadows in the glorious now. But in a month, or year, she'll realise: remission is not health.

The rain falls faster, heavier; it feels like we're submerged. Outside is a smeared grey; only the road seems solid. True and straight and sure of purpose. On and on it goes.

Briefly – perhaps for air – their mouths disengage. Then she starts to speak. At first he smiles, but then his eyes start jerking sideways. Perhaps she's saying she's unhappy. That she's so alone. Whatever she's saying, it's heartfelt and true, and he is unprepared. He leans back, not far, but still the point is made. He has refused her trust.

Number of miles to Stockton: 20. He is looking out the window; she stares at the floor.

If only he'd touch her head or shoulder. That is all it would take. Then she'd lift her head and I'd say, 'It's alright. Please go on.'

I drive the bus. The rain falls hard. Other vehicles approach or retreat and I cannot see people in them. It's like when I'm driving at night: sometimes, when I'm very tired, I wonder if we're dead. If there was some great accident we have all forgotten.

Number of miles to the San Joaquin bridge: 10. I push on the gas. The needle glides from 50 to 60. Dominique's head stays down.

Number of miles to the bridge: 8. In the distance, above Stockton, there is a rent in the cloud. As we approach, it seems to widen; then the sun breaks through. The road is a strip that shines and beckons. We reach 65.

Number of miles to the bridge: 6. 'Driver,' says a young guy in front, and there is concern in his voice. 'Yeah?' I say, and then he swallows, says, 'Aren't we going too fast?' 'It's fine,' I say and he sits back. We reach 70. Now the passengers are anxious; they lean and confer. Some of them must be decent people who mow their lawns, pay their taxes, recycle plastic and glass. Unfortunately, this makes no difference. It is not a question of worth.

Number of miles to the bridge: 4. The sky is clear, the sun is bright. The view, in those final seconds, will be incredible.

Number of men who have stood up: 3. They stagger down the aisle. 'Fuck are you doing?' says one. 'Slow the fuck *down*,' says another. They are blocking the rear view mirror. I yell at them to move. 'Call 9-1-1,' a woman says, and suddenly I'm scared. Not for myself, but Dominique. Is this just to punish her? Is there no other way?

They rattle the door. They hit the glass. The bridge is now in sight. I turn the wheel hard to the left and 2 of the men fall.

Number of people talking on phones: 17. The girl is on her boyfriend's lap. Screams and shaking heads and tears and hands entwined in prayer. Dominique is the only one who doesn't look afraid. Her arms are tight round the bearded man's neck. Although their faces are close, they are not kissing, just staring into each other's eyes. His chin trembles, he speaks, she smiles. They are like the lovers' shadows found on a Japanese wall. So united, so *together*, they left an indelible mark.

And so I wrench the wheel to the right, step hard on the brake. But this is too little, too late. We hit the side at 45 and there is a long moment when I gaze downriver. As far as the bend, the Louis Park, the Golf and Country Club. The sun goads the water to blue; roads are substitute rivers.

Then, after the shock of impact: cries of panic, pain. The windshield is completely gone. Blood on my hands and face.

'Go to the back,' I shout, and surprisingly they do. They huddle and gasp and cry while I remain at the front. Soon there'll be police and sirens; many kinds of relief. She will cry and he will hold her. This is how it will be.

I allow myself one final glance. Then I am following the water's great push. Bend after bend, through the False River, along the New York Slough. Down the Carquinez Straight, into the San Pablo bay. A pause to gather will and then. On to the Pacific. To its horizon without feature. Its waves beyond count.

The Slope

Miss Adams asked what she'd been practicing. Ruth began to play, arms extended, back straight, while Miss Adams sat. They stayed that way for seven minutes, neither noticing the kitchen sounds (plate on plate, some solid *chops*) or from further, in the yard, the back and forth of Daddy's saw on the dead elm tree.

Ruth sounded the last D sharp, let the key rise with her finger. The note lodged in the walls and floor, in the cameo at Miss Adams' throat. It curled and got comfy.

Ruth counted three, four, had got to six when Miss Adams said, 'You began that well.' She blushed, because Miss Adams meant this as a compliment. Beginnings were very important to her: if things were going to finish well, they had to start out right.

Of course Miss Adams said other things. That Chopin had not meant the middle part to be a race; that she had got two bars confused (and here Miss Adams stood and walked to the piano, and this was a rare privilege, because she did not usually like to play). She ended, as she often did, by saying, 'It is not just the notes. There is also the *feeling*.'

But Ruth knew she *had* done well, because then Miss Adams asked what she would like to learn next. And although this wasn't a real question, Ruth answered truthfully. Miss Adams looked out the window, where the sky and few remaining leaves calmly returned her gaze. It would be a good sunset, one, perhaps, to watch.

Miss Adams said, 'No. That's too difficult.' Because of course there was an order, a sequence to learning, and you could not jump this queue any more than you could start to climb a mountain from halfway.

Ruth nodded, said, 'Yes, Miss Adams.' She did not protest that she had already bought the music. If Miss Adams said the piece was too hard, she was certainly right.

*

At school Ruth was told about the First World War. Mr Matthews paced and spoke of trenches, gas, who was on who's side. He said, 'Never before had people died in their millions.' He sounded angry about it.

After lunch Carmen told her she had a crush on Luke. 'Why?' said Ruth and Carmen replied she liked the shape of his nose.

Ruth's hair was still damp from the pool when she set off for home. Wind hurried the smaller clouds and bent the branches back. The sky was purple slashed as she entered the park. She smelt the smoke of leaf bonfires and turned right at the swings. And she had heard the Ashkenazy recording, its haste and its precision. It was difficult, but surely, it couldn't hurt to try.

So after dinner, after grammar, Ruth opened the forbidden score. She smoothed her eyes from left to right, felt her fingers tense. She read on, past the opening, through the first climb, to the movement's end. Her teeth pressured her lips. She thought she maybe could. The problem would be the changes, they looked way too fast.

But when Ruth went downstairs then into the small room where the piano waited with such patience, this was not the piece she started. Instead she began the Liszt Miss Adams had prescribed. She made mistakes – sharps not flats, missed and added notes – but carried on regardless. That way she had the whole of it, not perfect little parts. She played it twice more, each time working on the problems, tugging at the knots. She liked it, it was nice. But it didn't matter.

*

She woke to the sound of rain, a gentle pattering. She had been on the beach; swimming in the ocean. That was all she could remember, and when her mother knocked, three soft raps, Ruth said she was awake. She got up, washed her face, combed her brown hair smooth.

When she entered the kitchen her father said, 'Good

morning.' Her mother was boiling eggs. Ruth buttered her toast and then her mother gave them their eggs. When Ruth removed the top of hers, it smelt of baby birds, the fume cupboards from Chemistry. She said she wasn't hungry, that she would be late. After a lecture, then a glass of milk, she was allowed to leave.

It wasn't real rain. Apart from the roads – black and shiny – there wasn't much, not enough for umbrellas. As she walked to school, past the old church, past the sweet shop, all the car tyres said *shush*. She thought of the opening bars. And when Mr Webb asked someone to draw the stamen and pistil, while she kept watch as Carmen tried to steal make-up, Ruth saw the notes, her hands.

But her hands had to be washed. They had to lay the table. They had to be folded for grace; to hold the knife that cut the meatloaf that was just okay. They had to draw the Niger delta; graph the mean expenditure of farmers B and C. Finally, just after nine, Ruth descended the stairs softly, almost on tiptoe. She heard a news voice say, *nuclear*, her father's quick answer. She closed the thick door, raised the wooden lip. She sat, opened the score, then sat some more, her pulse quicker, her ears working hard. So long as she was practicing, her mother (who only knew a little Schubert) wouldn't say anything. Ruth straightened and began.

*

The sun sliced through, a late fly buzzed, baffled but resigned.

She woke. She yawned and stretched in a happy, not-a-school-day manner. She thought, *If I had a cat, would it be here now? What would it be called?*

A smell of smoke, the woody kind, brought her to the window. Her father, his lips pursed, was sweeping, burning leaves. Ruth yawned again. She had played long after her bedtime, and if it had been reading or TV, they would have said something.

The fly started to sound pathetic. She lifted the window, tried to shoo it out. It recoiled from the cold air, made for the warm centre. And the beginning was definitely a problem: a downhill with no brakes; so steep it was falling.

Ruth heard her name called. 'Honey, we're going shopping.' She heard her reply, the pause, then the door shutting. The engine started, and she stood, hearing the sound recede. Ruth put on her dressing gown; pushed her feet into slippers; softly padded downstairs.

A tap was dripping in the kitchen where the chrome was gleaming. She poured herself some milk, drank half of it, then refilled the glass. The piano room was as she'd left it, the lid up, the score on the stand. She turned to the first page. And even though she knew this part, her eyes joined the dots. Perhaps she had missed something. But no, these were all the notes; the way that it should sound.

So she tried again, cautiously, her hands trying to think ahead, her legs a little cold. At first things were fine, her fingers ran but managed to keep pace. She was halfway down when she stumbled, and when that happened, she looked back, then down, which made her falter more; by the bottom of the page her confidence was bruised.

But she had been trained to play on, to not quit when behind. She slipped, she lurched, but eventually, the piece began to level off and then, as if emerging from a ravine, things started to open. The notes began to flow and merge; their torrent slowed to a stream. Ruth walked along its looping banks, through a lush, well-watered valley, the sun spring-bright, the slow stream purling on. Her fingers followed the course, its grand meander, gentle sweeps, the lazy snake of it. Then the key bit through the lock, and there were feet and voices. She started, loudly said, 'I'm here.' The feet approached. 'Heavens, you're not even dressed.' She half turned. 'Sorry, I've been practicing.' Her mother said, 'Well, that's good,' while her father, unseen, looked to God.

On Sunday they went for a drive. They had a picnic; sat in what was left of fall; wood-walked on the leaf carpet; met other families and dogs. Ruth walked behind her parents, looking at the scattered silver, fallen gold: the devalued currency of 1969.

Then it was back to school. On Monday she had orchestra. They were warned about a charity concert. They practiced The Thieving Magpie.

When she got home she was tired and had a lot of French.

She did not attempt the piece next day either. She did not lack the time (Math had been cancelled), or the inclination.

It was because she had her lesson tomorrow. If she practiced it now her efforts might leave a trace, an echo that the highly trained ear of Miss Adams might catch. And if she knew that Ruth had disobeyed her, attempted peaks as well as hills, she would say (as she had on the only occasion when Ruth was unprepared) how *very* disappointed she was. So Ruth did not try the descent again. Instead she tinkled out the Liszt, its little chirping sounds. She worked hard on it, made progress, so much that Miss Adams spoke of her playing it in the winter county contest. But despite all this, despite having done nothing wrong, Ruth was happy when the clock chimed eight and Miss Adams stood.

*

The first snow fell at dawn, piling fast enough to evoke cries of wonder, shakes of head. Milk was heated, hats put on, and then the flakes abruptly stopped without a by your leave. The sky began to clear, to blue; the sun said *false alarm.*

Ruth walked along the curb, wondering what shape her body would make; would there be a general flattening or just a Ruth-shaped hole? Meanwhile the spades bit and scraped, clearing paths, preserving the old ways.

And why couldn't she play that piece? It wasn't impossible. Many people could. Six weeks, and still she fell each time. Sometimes she got in sight of the river's coils. But that was when she'd lose her footing, when her hands would trip.

She stepped over a patch of ice; heard distant shouts of throwing. She would only play the beginning. Only when she had that right, only after a proper descent; only then would she allow herself to walk beside the stream.

The bell was ringing when she got to school. Ruth knocked the snow from her shoes then went inside, down the corridor, into her homeroom. Carmen was there already, and Sue-Anne, and Lucille, and Miss Fender in two sweaters, looking up, making a green tick next to *Ruth*.

The room filled. A second bell rang. Miss Fender said, 'All of you should pay attention. Today's assembly will be special.' Then she stood up, walked towards the door, and they all did the same. They filed out, turned left, walked down the corridor. They curved round to the right, a little troop not quite in step, Miss Fender leading, thinking *Bob should buy another.*

They entered the hall and walked past rows of orange chairs. When they reached the black chairs they sat and this was the signal for Mrs Gramm to start. And for the first few notes Ruth was convinced that she was playing *her* piece, and nothing would have been more unfair. To have to hear her mangle pieces she knew she could play better; this was bad enough. But for her to somehow be able to play a piece so obviously beyond her, for this to be the rule's exception: this would be too much.

But no, old Gramm was just rushing the allegro of the Greig in G. Ruth folded her hands and watched the other classes enter. The orange filled, and then the black. The hall was bright with chatter. Then the principal came forward and a hush descended. She said, 'Today we are very fortunate.' She gestured to a man dressed as a soldier, his hair the same grey as their skirts, his face kind and strict. Mrs Gramm began to play All Things Bright and Beautiful and they all stood up. They sang the happy song. Afterwards the soldier asked them to take a good long look out the window. He said, 'Some of your brothers and fathers are there. And there's no snow where they are.'

Then he asked them to lower their heads and pray and they did as they were told.

*

Miss Adams had never missed a Wednesday. Not for the dentist, not for the hairdresser; not when her sister from Vermont had finally come to visit. Not even when she sliced the tip of her left pinkie. Then she had been pale and digit wrapped, but present nonetheless. So when Ruth's mother said at breakfast, 'Honey, Miss Adams can't make it tonight,' Ruth felt her tone was wrong. This was not clothes left on the floor, not what book was she reading.

'Why not?'

'I'm not sure. She didn't say. Probably she's busy. She teaches other girls you know.'

'How many?'

'I don't know. Maybe five or six. Anyway, she'll be back next week. You can have a rest.'

She'd practiced for nothing. Who'd hear it if not Miss Adams? Mom and Dad?

But no, she thought. It might be useful. There were fast passages, not as rapid as that opening drop, but still swift, and in one place, quite steep. Maybe she could borrow from them, find something to help.

On Wednesday morning they played rounders and she hurt her knee. After this Mr Matthews told them of the Great Depression. Carmen was sent to the office. In the afternoon they had a test Ruth didn't think she'd pass.

She was in the piano room when the clock struck six. She sat there until quarter past, a sick sensation ticking through her. Then she pretended that Miss Adams had asked. Ruth reached out, G sharp, F flat, fingers roaming, pressing out the notes. It moved in a stately fashion, occasionally darting forward, always settling back. And though it wasn't valleys, streams, at the end she did feel better. And it was as if the sounds had waited for her to finish: the front door shut, the mowers ran, dogs began to bark. She heard the stair creak, a carpet being beaten. She took the score from her bag.

She smoothed it over the Grieg. She lowered her hands. Then stopped. Because this was lesson time.

But there would be a week for it to fade (assuming Miss Adams was not too busy). So she bit her lip and started, and again she fell, early, badly, her foot-fingers twisted in the space between. She couldn't even listen to the Ashkenazy: his ease was someone running, laughing, shouting, look at *me*. Ruth wanted to tear it up, scatter and un-join its dots. But there was still the middle, its slow stream. It was like the answers in the back of the textbook: the problem was how to reach them.

*

Winter warmed into spring. Miss Adams returned, but now she only came every two weeks. And though she still spoke of Beginnings, she had new words too: *potential; promise; improvement.* Such talk made Ruth blush and wonder if she could say *Now do you think I am ready?*, But before she dared to ask things came to an end. One day she got home and found that her mother had made her favourite. After Ruth finished her mother said 'Honey, I have good news.' And Ruth sat and listened, and although her mother saw her eyes moisten, she didn't see her cry. That happened ten minutes later, in the warm hug of her sheets. That Miss Adams was getting married, this was strange, she was too old. But for her to move to Kansas, with a builder, this she could not accept.

That summer she read. She lay on the porch. She went to Church Youth Camp where someone almost drowned. She helped her mother. She followed the old train tracks until she got tired. And while she did these things, the dust on the piano smiled; began to feel settled.

The holidays ended. Leaves began to turn as breath began to smoke. Carmen said she'd had a boyfriend who had taken her to third base. Ruth's mother said she was having trouble finding a replacement. But she should practise anyway, go over old pieces.

And so the dust was scattered, flung into a diaspora of the walls and corners. Ruth sat down with Liszt and Chopin, with Grieg and Debussy. One by one she propped them open, tried to play despite the quivering in her stomach. Although she made few mistakes, none of it felt right. She felt like something hollow that had been struck hard.

She rested her hands on the keys. The sun entered the room. She pictured Miss Adams in Kansas, watching her husband build houses and saying *You began that well.*

Ruth pulled the score from the pile. She turned past the opening – even that brief glimpse produced a sense of vertigo – kept turning till she heard the river's liquid song. As she played the stream was chrome bright, silver scrawled on green. She wound with it through the valley, followed each meander. It was dizzying; she felt surrounded; wholly embraced by sound. When she finished, when the stream vanished, she began again.

Because – and she was sure of this – the main thing was to play. Miss Adams would never know. The slope could surely wait.

The Curve of the Heavens

A ten-year-old girl is trapped in the back of a van speeding out of the city. Sally had been at a birthday party where there were baby rabbits and an old man played the accordion. She was having a lovely time until the man who brought the rabbits put her in his van and drove away. Now Sally is in a lot of trouble. Things do not look good. But suddenly the driver has pains in his chest and has to stop by the side of the road. His vision darkens. He cannot breathe. The last thing he sees is Sally's face in the rear view mirror. She has orange cheeks and black lines radiating from both sides of her mouth. The make up is smeared because she has been a scared little tiger.

When Sally sees the bad man slump it takes her a moment to understand. Then she starts banging on the side of the van. The noise of her small fists on the metal is surprisingly loud. She doesn't have to wait long before the door slides open with a sound that's like a roar. Sally's saviour is a middle-aged Caucasian woman wearing sunglasses even though the sky is overcast.

'My goodness,' she says. 'What's happened to you? And who is this man?' Sally is too overcome to speak, but the woman answers her silence. 'Never mind. Let's get you some help.'

Sally is so relieved. She climbs awkwardly out the van, her small limbs stiff after her captivity. She stares up at the woman's curiously nondescript face and waits for her rescuer to introduce herself and tell Sally what to do next. But the woman does not say her name. She does not ask Sally's address or take out her phone and call the police. And even a ten-year-old finds this strange. But there are no houses or shops in view; the only buildings are giant metal sheds without windows. There is no one else who can help.

'Come with me,' the woman says and starts to walk away from the road. Sally follows her down a narrow lane by the side of one of the metal sheds that is littered with small pieces of white polystyrene that resemble fragments of brain. On one side there's a high blank wall, on the other metal railings fence off a canal. The woman points to a gap in the fence.

'We'll go this way,' she says and Sally hesitates. The woman bends down and says 'What's wrong?' and her breath smells so much like old milk it makes Sally flinch. The woman no longer seems like the benevolent stranger who was supposed to escort Sally back to her mother. After her ordeal in the van she hasn't much trust in strangers. When the woman extends a reassuring hand Sally steps away then ducks through the hole in the fence. She runs along the canal. She goes under a bridge and then it's dark and her footsteps are explosions. When she emerges she sees two teenage boys, one on a mountain bike, the other on foot. As she approaches the boy on the bike says something that makes his friend laugh. Both become serious when they see how upset Sally is.

'What's happened?,' says the boy on foot, who has bright ginger hair, very thick glasses, and is named Mike. Mike looks completely trustworthy, as does his friend Tim. Both have solid, decent faces that suggest a good upbringing.

'Someone's chasing me,' says Sally, then turns around. She and the boys stare into the dark of the bridge for a long time but no one appears.

If Mike and Tim were less nice they might suggest that Sally was making the whole thing up. But they believe her.

'Come on, let's find your mum,' says Mike. Tim agrees, then says 'Let's go to my house, it's closer.' They walk and over the next few minutes they find out Sally's name, where she lives, what school she goes to. During this time neither boy says or does anything suspicious. Sally starts to relax. She wants to believe she is now safe. The only problem is that I can't help remembering a news story about a boy lured by two older boys to a deserted stretch of canal. This was where they beat him, though not where he died, and the similarity between that scenario and Sally's situation means I can't help drawing parallels. And no doubt those killers were friendly at first. Mike and Tim could be just as bad. The only way for Sally to be safe is for something to change.

'What?' says Mike and drops his bike and Tim just stares. Instead of a little girl there is now a young woman with smeared make up and clothes that are incredibly tight.

'It's OK,' says Sally. Although she doesn't understand what's happened, she likes the change. She's stronger and more confident. She can protect herself.

I realise this transformation may complicate things for you as a reader. It is one thing for me to stop a heart: that happens all the time in both real and fictional worlds. But someone ageing nine years in a second is the kind of thing that only happens in worlds that make no claim to being 'realistic'.

'Do you still need our help?' Mike asks, and although Sally doesn't think so, she still says, 'Yes, please.' And so they walk on. By the time they reach a bus stop both boys have a harmless crush on this pretty young woman who is smart, funny and cannot wait to get to university to study Physics. She can name the constellations. She loves to swing dance. She is excellent at rolling joints and almost never loses at pool. She's also skipped over a lot of bad things that would probably have happened. Teenage pregnancies, teenage heartbreak; the divorce of her parents; the death of a parent; falling in with a bad, drug-using, shoplifting crowd; being stalked by a psycho killer while at summer camp. In this world the lives of teenagers are like the surface of a lake that is never allowed to be calm.

It's almost dark by the time Sally gets home. At first her mother doesn't believe that the tall young woman with smeared orange cheeks is her daughter, a daughter who should've been home hours ago. She has been so worried. Perhaps this is why she eventually accepts this impossible transformation –

better this than never see Sally again. But there must be some other reason why she, those nice boys, and everyone Sally knows is willing to believe the unbelievable. They actually seem pleased. Sally's father – who had been depressed – now whistles as he walks. Her friends at school, who were previously average, become the hardest working students in their year. Word spreads, posts are shared, tweets retweeted, until #MIRACLEGIRL is trending on every kind of social media. After a week the news is almost entirely about Sally because nothing much else is happening. All the conflicts have ended. Nobody is killing, stealing, taking hostages, having sex with people they shouldn't. It has been the most peaceful, uneventful week in the history of this world. Which is wonderful, really great. Though perhaps a little dull.

This situation lasts a month. Then Russia annexes a Baltic state. There are forest fires, new diseases, twenty-seven earthquakes. Leonardo Di Caprio's head is found in a tartan suitcase on a dirt road in Montana. And as normal life resumes its procession of tragedy and drama, Sally starts her Astrophysics degree at Imperial College London. She really likes her professors. Her roommates are great. At night her sleep is dreamless.

Five years pass. All dogs are feral. The skies of Germany and France are full of mostly harmless meteorites. But 23 year-old Sally is in no danger in Brighton where she lives in a flat overlooking the sea. She's in a relationship with Daichi, a kind, tubby man from Shanghai who's doing his PhD in the same department as her. On Sundays they take long walks on the Sussex Downs without picking a path. They prefer to be guided by the landscape. Following the line of a ridge or a stream's curves is better than picking a destination.

In a less bumpy world this would be a lovely idea. But for them there must always be obstacles. A barbed wire fence, a Keep Out sign, the revelation that Daichi has a neurodegenerative disease so rare it doesn't appear on Google. He'll be paralysed by the time he's 30. No one with this condition has ever lived beyond 40. Daichi is impressively calm after his diagnosis.

'Ever since I was a child I've thought something like this would happen to me,' he says. 'It's just what God does. Some people have to die early or the world could not go on.'

Sally is less phlegmatic. Her own difficulties have given her a keener sense of empathy than is usual in someone her age. When she thinks about what lies ahead for Daichi she cries and asks herself all the usual futile questions about Why Terrible Things Happen to Good People. I also find this upsetting. I'd hoped their relationship would go on much longer, admittedly for selfish reasons: it's exhausting to have to keep intervening.

But apart from his fatal condition, their life together is great. After Sally completes her PhD she is offered a job at Cambridge University. She writes a best-selling book about black holes that one reviewer describes as 'the Harry Potter of popular science.' She uses the money to buy a small cottage in a village so quaintly English – its thatched houses drip with roses; cricket is played on the village green – it seems more like a film set than a real place. She gets a rescue dog – a lurcher named Mitzi – and every morning she and Daichi get up early to walk the gentle hound for an hour. For six months the three of them lead a life of such contentment it should qualify as her end.

But to finish here would be irresponsible. To abandon Sally in this world, age 27, would be like leaving a child in a city centre overnight. And while it may seem both wrong and belittling to compare a capable and confident young woman to a child, let me stress that in this world any of us, all of us, would be equally defenceless. There's still so much that can happen to Sally. I don't need to list the possibilities; you'll have your own ideas.

It all happens too quickly. One morning Sally wakes and finds Daichi on the bathroom floor. He cannot move his legs. He has been quietly crying for hours. In hospital they inject his legs with corticosteroids and within a day he can walk again. But the doctor says that by the end of the year he'll need to use a wheelchair. The following day neither of them go to work. They take a picnic and follow the curves of the woods to Devil's Dyke then rise to Ditchling Beacon. From that high vantage point the hedges, roads and fences that divide the countryside seem like desperate attempts to join a set of hidden dots. If there is a pattern, nobody can see it.

They remain there until sunset, sometimes kissing, but not saying much.

The air is cooling when they start to descend. In the gloaming, in that golden hour, they walk hand in hand. Two weeks later he will stand on the deck of a ferry and watch the sun calmly descend. His last thought, just as he steps off, is that his death has meaning.

For the next three years Sally grieves. She tells people that she doesn't want to meet someone new. She was in love, but now that is over, and can never happen again. At first glance this may seem a problem. How is Sally supposed to find true happiness – which of course requires another person – if she is determined to be alone? Eventually I must figure this out, but for now there is no rush. Dating is so risky. Even if that other person isn't crazy, jealous, controlling, deceitful, manipulative or cruel – and who doesn't have the potential to be those things? – they will have family, friends, colleagues and ex-lovers who can be just as dangerous.

And although Sally is in mourning she's not always unhappy. There are moments when she feels as warmly illuminated as someone emerging from a dark cellar into noon sunshine. It doesn't take much. The scent of lilies; the eyes of a dog; the brightness of wet tarmac. These things anchor her to a present that seems worthwhile. She has her research, she travels often – though only in Britain, and never by plane – and she has a small group of friends she sees most weekends. If I have not mentioned them before it is only because it was safer to leave them vague. Suffice to say that they are all happily married, most with children, and although one or two of them may have a crush on their miraculous friend they lack the courage to act on it. Only after two bottles of Prosecco will Becky's eyes frankly consider the heft of Sally's breasts. Hopefully this won't be a problem; there is certainly some risk.

Nothing much changes for Sally during the next five years. Though this time is not uneventful for her, none of these happenings are the usual stuff of fiction. I certainly would not like to read a story about the pleasure someone gets from taking up swimming at their local pool. Nor would I be interested in a story about a person deciding to change their consumer behaviour to reduce their carbon footprint. I suppose there could be *some* interest in the story of a young woman spending a month at a powerful telescope high in the Andes with only a half-blind technician and a tortoise for company, but there was neither an unlikely romance nor dangerous tension between them. He imparted no wisdom. Sally took measurements, did calculations, and read a lot of novels that were neither inspirational nor transformative. When she walked beneath bright stars she had no revelations.

I'd go so far as to say that during these five years Sally, though the star of this story, has the least interesting life of anyone in her world. Infidelity, domestic abuse, sexual dysfunction, the loss of a child, a miscarriage, an inability to conceive, one partner loving the other too much, neither partner loving each other, the growing tendency of one partner to insult the other while talking in their sleep: these are only some of the problems facing the couples she knows. As for the single people of her acquaintance, their lives are no better. Most are nursing issues from their adolescence that make them so unhappy and insecure they exist in a constant state of low level anxiety. Though these people are generally functional – i.e. they have jobs and buy stuff – they regularly find themselves in challenging and unlikely situations that lead them to do or say something with painful or terrible consequences. He blurts out racist comments. She defaces a painting. They run over a child.

Sally's friends like to joke about how easy her life is. 'I bet you don't even get wet when it rains,' says Becky when Sally visits her in hospital.

'Oh come on,' she answers, then smiles, but is embarrassed by her good luck. She doesn't know why she is being spared. I guess I don't know either. I've hurt or killed so many characters; all of them could have been saved.

Becky's funeral takes place on a July morning so spectacularly fine it seems to mock the occasion. The handles of her coffin sparkle. As her remains are lowered her husband Neil twists his head away. This cannot be happening. His vision is blurred by tears, his eyes cannot focus. When they recover he sees other grieving faces, all of which he passes over until he gets to Sally. Although she looks as upset as everyone else, and he has never had a bad thought about her – she never encouraged Becky

– Neil suddenly loathes this fucking bitch that nothing ever touches. She doesn't belong in this world. He enjoys this hatred for ten seconds before his grief smothers it. For the next six months he's too depressed and sick with mourning to exhume the thought. But eventually, after four pints, Neil shares it with a mutual friend.

'There's something not right with Sally,' he tells Dave. They are celebrating Dave's release from prison for a crime he did not commit.

'You mean apart from having a decade missing from her life? I've never understood that. I used to think it was a hoax. But there's a lot of weird shit in this world that doesn't make any sense. Still, you're right. Something's going on.'

And in this way, by conversation, and by text, a consensus builds among her friends. Sally is hiding something. Exactly what they can't put into words – it would sound too ridiculous – but this secret, if she shared it, might protect them as well. When Neil takes her out for dinner on her birthday (her 36th, or 27th) he is dropping hints before the main course arrives.

'I'm sorry I didn't get you a present. But what do you get for the woman who has everything?'

Sally laughs. 'If only. I can think of plenty of things I'm missing.'

Neil fashions a smile, but when he says, 'Like what?' it comes from a tight throat.

'Well, I'm terminally single for one thing. And I didn't get that dream job I applied for in New Orleans.' (Because in

2016 that otherwise wonderful city had the seventh-highest number of shootings in the US).

Neil shrugs. 'It's all relative. I wish I had your problems.'

There isn't much Sally can say to this. Him finding out recently that he was adopted was obviously a blow; but to then discover his adoptive parents had killed his real father and mother was as unbearable as it was unbelievable. What with all this, and Becky's death, Neil has every right to feel aggrieved. Sally starts to apologise – as if it were her fault! – but Neil talks over her sympathy.

'I mean, don't you think it's remarkable? You're the only person I know who doesn't have something awful to deal with.'

Plates of fish arrive. They accept potatoes. When the waitress has gone Sally says, with quiet anger, 'I was abducted. My boyfriend killed himself. I'm sorry if you think that isn't enough misery.'

And most people would back off because she's right: in some ways I have failed to protect her. But one of Neil's crippling migraines is approaching. The pain is licking his mind. He has little time to find a fresh angle.

'Just tell me,' he says. 'Are you some kind of alien? Do you have magical powers or a guardian angel?'

She laughs and tells him he's crazy. But of course she has wondered. She's walked down dark alleys at night just to see if anything would happen. But she's never tested the idea properly. She's never crossed the road without looking or jumped off a bridge. So she makes no reply. They eat and look at their phones. They do not have dessert.

Although Sally has survived this encounter, things are looking ominous. I will have to grit my teeth and imagine a stable, decent, honest, considerate partner for Sally, someone who comes from a loving family, gets on well with their exes, has no criminal record, no stalkers, no fatal diseases, no sexual hang ups, but who is still attractive and interesting enough to make Sally happy for the rest of her life. I must be a miracle worker.

On a balmy day in early September Sally is asleep on a train going from London to Edinburgh. The train has just curved out of Newcastle. When she closed her eyes the seat opposite was empty. But now, as she slowly wakes, a face is in front of her. It is not the kind of face you'll see on a glossy magazine cover. The nose has been broken. The mouth is tiny, the teeth crooked. The eyes are the disappointing grey that occurs when too many colours are mixed together. But these eyes are also inquisitive, lively and concentrating on her. Sally looks away, out the window, sees bungalows, a park, a tethered horse, then brings her gaze back to find the eyes are still looking at her.

The eyes remain on Sally as the person speaks. 'Do you want a coffee? It will be terrible. But I'm going to have one anyway.'

Without thinking, Sally says, 'Alright.' She does not consider – as she really should – that the person could put something in her coffee that will make her unconscious or kill her. I suppose this is what comes of leading a sheltered life.

And as Sally unaccountably blushes fifteen of her friends – two of them on crutches, one in a wheelchair – gather in a private room above a pub in Edinburgh. Some are meeting for the first time, so at first the conversation is taken up with introductions. They are finishing their first drink when Neil clears his throat.

'I think we all know why we're here. We need to do something about Sally.' And then, because he used to do corporate training, he divides them into small groups. 'You've got 20 minutes to brainstorm,' he says.

You cannot fall in love in 37 minutes, not even in this world. Love isn't what Sally feels as the train approaches Berwick-upon-Tweed. Wings are beating behind her eyes, there's fluttering in her stomach, a sense that she is expanding beyond her own borders. A wonderful, terrific feeling, but not love; not yet. As they arrive into town the stone walls of the harbour are two arms opening for an embrace. In their 37 minutes they haven't really spoken of much, just what they do and where they're from. The tone of their conversation is what makes Sally anxious about how little time they have left. They are speaking with the warmth and intimacy of people who have known each other their whole lives. Perhaps you or I might find it odd, even suspicious – must be something in the coffee – to feel such a powerful affinity for a complete stranger. All I can say is that occasionally things are better in this world.

The small groups report back. Neil summarises. 'So we have five options. Blackmail,' he says, then writes the word on the whiteboard. The other four options are *Exposure; Make her leave the country; Hire a private detective;* and *Get someone to hack her phone.*

'Aren't four and five more or less the same?' asks the man in the wheelchair. 'I mean, he'd do that wouldn't he?'

They debate this, then agree to combine these options. 'Alright,' says Neil. 'We now have four options. Shall we vote?'

As Sally tells her new friend about Daichi she keeps glancing at her watch. So little time remains. She would like to say *Why don't we go back to London?* That would give them another five hours together. In that time anything would be possible.

Sally is getting ready to say 'I really like you,' when the person (who I think is a woman) asks her for a pen. Sally is nonplussed, because it means the woman (who is called Kirsten) is thinking of something else, or *someone* else, but she looks through her bag until she finds a pen.

'Thanks,' says Kirsten then writes a sequence of numbers on the back of a receipt. 'This is my number. Call me.'

Sally nods, and this is all very promising, but too much can happen between when they get off the train and when they meet for their date.

'Wait,' says Kirsten. 'I've got a better idea. Let's go on a date as soon as we arrive.'

Sally's friends cannot decide between blackmail and making Sally leave the country. For twenty minutes they argue.

'I just don't see what good it would do to make her leave,'

says the man in the wheelchair (who looks like a Gary). 'Maybe whatever she's doing is affecting the whole world. You only have to look at the news to see everything's gone to shit.'

No one disagrees. But the vote remains tied. And then Neil realises someone hasn't voted. He looks around the room and sees Dave staring out the window.

'Dave, you're being very quiet. Don't you care?'

For a moment Dave does not respond. Then he sighs. 'I don't know why we're having to argue. It's really very simple. We just need to kill her.'

Kirsten can't decide where to go. 'I don't want this to be an ordinary date,' she says. 'We should go somewhere we've never been before.'

Sally nods, thinks a moment, says, 'What about somewhere you'd never usually consider going?'

Kirsten laughs. 'You mean somewhere terrible? Alright. I know the perfect place.'

A long silence follows Dave's suggestion. Some of them look shocked. Dave waits for someone to condemn him. A minute passes, then another. Gary has his face in his hands. His shoulders are shaking. The poor man has been through so much; no wonder he's breaking down. But the sound that sneaks between his palms is not a sob, but a laugh. He raises his head and says, 'Absolutely. And I know where she is. We can go do it right now.'

The train has stopped although I did not tell it to. The other passengers are grumbling into phones, jabbing at screens. Kirsten and Sally do not care. They are holding hands.

They know she's taking the train. They know what time it arrives. They have a very simple plan. They don't care if they are caught.

With a jolt, the train starts to move. Several people cheer. The suburbs of Edinburgh permit their entry.

Her former friends are in four taxis. Most of them have knives. Neil thinks

It will be like Julius Caesar. They will swarm around her. It will happen so fast then they'll be gone.

Sally and Kirsten unlock hands, pick up bags, step down from the train. When they are halfway down the platform they can see a small crowd at the arrival gate. Kirsten puts her hand on Sally's shoulder. 'Quick. Hide. It's the paparazzi.'

'Too late. Shall we give them something?' she says and leans in for a kiss. Their brief meeting of mouths makes small detonations plummet down Sally's spine. Her world is only two moist lips that faintly taste of lip gloss. She is giddy. She is in love.

Their kiss should go on forever but this world has its demands. Sally goes through the ticket barrier. She walks towards the waiting crowd while Kirsten hunts for her ticket. She wonders why so many of the people waiting have their backs turned to the gate. Just before she reaches them she stops and looks behind her. As she does Kirsten yells her name.

'What?' she says but it's too late. Kirsten has caught up. Together they make their way through the crowd. They have almost left the station when Kirsten takes her arm. 'Here we are. What do you think?'

Sally considers the station pub's metal chairs, overflowing ashtrays, its sweet reek of old beer. 'It's awful. It's perfect.'

Kirsten laughs then puts down her bags. 'Isn't it? Take a seat, I'll get the first round.' And so Sally sits down outside the station bar just as the four taxis arrive.

This is where the story could end. If I threw up my hands and abandoned Sally to the knives of her friends then the message, God help us, would be something to do with the difficulty of maintaining authorial intention in the face of the tropes and conventions of contemporary fiction. But while that may be true, it seems stupid to have rescued Sally from being sacrificed on one altar only to offer her up on another. At the same time I have to acknowledge that in this world there will always be assassins, whether walking or in wheelchairs. I can only think of one way to protect Sally from what I demand as a reader.

And so when the killers arrive they will be just in time to witness Sally and Kirsten disappearing. Neither they, nor anyone else, will ever see these women again. The place they are going to is a tiny world made only for them. The house they will live in is small, but snug. It is surrounded by fir trees. On the ground there is always snow but the two of them are never cold. The fire inside is cheerful and even though they never go out, because there is nowhere to go to, they are never bored. They dwell in a happy state they never want to end. The most excitement that enters their lives is when the little house begins to tremble. When this happens they do not worry; they calmly put down their books and go outside. Holding hands they look up into a sky that seems so close they can see the curve of the heavens. Snowflakes fall, then slowly settle. The snow will lie on the ground, in peace, until their globe shakes again.

Acknowledgements

'The Ballad of Poor Lucy Miller', 'The Embrace', 'Octet', 'And Then' all first appeared in The Southern Review.

'New Traffic Patterns May Emerge' first appeared in Short Fiction 10.

'Ward' won the Willesden Herald 2014 Short Story Prize.

'Half' first appeared in New Short Stories 6.

'The Slope' first appeared in New Writing Scotland.

'The False River' first appeared in The Manchester Review.

Nick Holdstock is the author of a novel, *The Casualties*, and three books of non-fiction: *The Tree That Bleeds*, *China's Forgotten People* and *Chasing the Chinese Dream*. He has written for the *London Review of Books*, the *Guardian*, *The Times Literary Supplement*, and *Financial Times*. He lives in Edinburgh.